Out of the Darkness

Michael Clinton Oliver

*To Bobby & Laura —
Nice to meet you at
the Cape. Best of luck
in the future.*

Llumina Press

*Michael O.
2010*

© 2007 Michael Clinton Oliver

All rights reserved. No part of this publication may be reproduced or transmitted in any form or by any means electronic or mechanical, including photocopy, recording, or any information storage and retrieval system, without permission in writing from both the copyright owner and the publisher.

Requests for permission to make copies of any part of this work should be mailed to Permissions Department, Llumina Press, PO Box 772246, Coral Springs, FL 33077-2246

ISBN:978-1-59526-690-3

Printed in the United States of America by Llumina Press

Library of Congress Control Number: 2007900414

Dedication

This book is dedicated to the memory of my stepson, Chase McGee (1986-2006).

You touched everyone's life that you met.
We love and miss you.

*It's not the length of a man's life,
but the breadth of his life that counts.*

Emerson

Prologue

Booneville, TN—Winter 1862

The riders came down the lane at daybreak. The rays of the sun were beginning to streak over the mountains, and wisps of fog still clung to the ground. The lead rider spurred his mare into a full gallop. A big, heavily built man weighing over 250 lbs, he seemed too large for his mount, though the horse stood sixteen hands high. A mixture of frost and snow covered the limbs of the ancient oak trees that lined the narrow road and meshed eerily with the cold breath of the horses.

A ragtag bunch of men followed close behind, their hats pulled down on their heads and the collars of their blue jackets turned up to protect against the piercing north wind. At the top of the hill, they slowed to a walk and drew their weapons.

Jim Patton rushed out of the barn when he heard the sound of hoof beats. He thought about running to the house, but the riders were too close. He slipped back into the shadows near the smokehouse and waited.

There wasn't much for them to steal this time. He had taken his gray mule and a jersey cow and hidden them in the hollow. He had a few bags of corn to feed them and maybe enough to plant in the spring. Everything else had been plundered in previous raids.

The big man reigned in his horse and dismounted. At his signal, the other men spread out around the white three-story house. "We want Josh Patton, and we want him now," the man shouted.

Inside the house, Nancy Patton hurried to the window. The group of men had completely encircled her house. Jim must be at the barn, she thought. He always got up early and went to get fresh milk for breakfast. Her oldest daughter, Sarah, came into the room so quietly that Nancy was frightened when she spoke. "What do those men want?" Sarah asked.

"That's Harley Brady and a bunch of his bushwhackers. They want your brother and whatever they can steal."

"Where's Papa?"

"He must be in the barn. Get the kids up and get them dressed warm."

Sarah left without replying. She reached her sister Beth's room, slipped inside, and woke her. Beth's husband Rob had been killed at Fort Donelson. It was too dangerous for her to be on her own with a two-year-old and a nine-month-old baby. She'd moved in with her parents after being attacked by a runaway slave.

"Send him out, or we'll burn the damn place down," Brady bellowed in a deep baritone voice.

"He ain't here," Jim Patton said, stepping out to where he could be seen.

Brady walked over to Jim, his gun drawn, but held across his chest. Where the hell is he?" Brady spat and wiped the tobacco juice on his sleeve.

"We ain't seen him in months."

"We heard he was here just a week ago."

"Why didn't you come looking then?" Jim asked. None of Brady's men said anything. "Maybe cause General Forrest was around these parts, and you was in hiding."

Infuriated, Brady drew his right hand back to strike Jim with the butt of his pistol. With cat-like quickness for a sixty-five-year-old man, Jim blocked the blow with his left arm and landed a right to Brady's face. Before he could strike again, one of Brady's men clubbed Jim in the back of the head with a rifle.

Nancy Patton ran down the stairs and out the door. One of Brady's men caught her and slung her back against the wall.

"Git everybody out of the house," Brady ordered. His men moved through the house with caution. They rounded up Sarah, Beth, and the children and ushered them outside. The icy wind stung their faces, and they shivered from the cold.

"I said I want Josh Patton, and I want him now!" Brady shouted.

He walked in front of the women and children and stopped next to Beth. He pressed his face close to her. She tried to turn her face, but Brady grabbed her by the hair. His breath smelled of stale coffee.

"Leave her alone!" Sarah shouted.

Brady ignored her and pushed Beth against the wall, his massive frame pinning her until she was unable to move. Sarah rushed Brady and grabbed his arm. He shoved her to the ground.

"Damn, Hoss," one of Brady's men shouted. "This one is a wildcat!" The men laughed, but Sarah scrambled off the ground and lunged at Brady once more. This time she ducked when Brady swung his arm, moved between Brady and her sister, and swung her right hand as hard as she could. Her fist caught Brady in the mouth with a resounding thud. "Damn bitch!" he yelled, spitting blood.

He let go of Beth and grabbed his face. Sarah swung again, but Brady was ready. He caught her arm with his left hand and slapped her with his right. Sarah tumbled to the ground, and Brady moved toward her.

"You're mine, little girl," he said, spitting blood on the ground. He grabbed Sarah by the hair and began to drag her toward the house.

The sound of a shot stopped him short of the door.

"Let her go, Brady!" the man who fired the shot yelled. "We're after Josh Patton, not a bunch of women."

Brady eyed the men on horseback. The captain still had his pistol in his hand, and his men had their rifles ready. No use pushing the issue, especially when the odds weren't in his favor.

"Yessir, Captain," Brady yelled, but still held Sarah by the hair. "What you want us to do? They have been hiding Forrest and them other damn rebels."

"Make the old man talk. String him up to that hickory tree and see what he has to say."

"I knowed I liked you for some reason, Captain Scruggs," Brady replied, relishing the idea of hanging Jim Patton.

Two of Brady's men picked Jim off the ground and tied his hands behind his back. Another man threw a noose over a limb and fastened the other end to his saddle horn. They tied a noose around Jim's neck, and the man began to back his horse up. Jim staggered for a moment then was lifted off the ground until only the tips of his toes touched. He danced on his toes, attempting to find solid footing. He tried to curse, but the rope cut off his air. He struggled, but was hoisted off the ground. The rider loosed the rope, and he crumbled to the earth.

Instantly, the two men were at his side, picking him up out of the mud. "Where's Josh Patton?" Brady yelled.

"Go to hell, Brady!" Jim said his voice barely audible. The rider reined his horse, yanking Jim off his feet, the rope tearing into the flesh of his neck. Three more times they repeated the process. Jim, unable to talk, shook his head defiantly.

"Leave him hanging this time," Brady ordered.

Sarah ran to the horse where the officer sat watching. "Captain Scruggs," she pleaded. "Please stop this. We expect this from a bushwhacker like Brady, but you're a Union soldier."

"Just tell us where Josh Patton is, and we will leave you alone," the officer said sternly.

"He's with the general. We don't know where they are. Last time we heard, they were in Beersheba Springs, but that was over a week ago. I swear to God that's the truth."

Captain Scruggs looked at her and nodded his head, satisfied that they had learned all they were going to from the Pattons. "Cut him down!" he ordered.

Brady looked stunned. "Ain't you going to make him talk?"

"We've found out all we are going to here. Mount up!"

Brady and his men reluctantly followed. After they moved away, the women rushed to Jim's side. Jim made several feeble attempts to speak and lapsed into unconsciousness.

Chapter 1

Bobby Jack Morris sped down the gravel road toward Dry Creek Bridge. A trail of dust snaked its way around the curves behind him. His hands shook nervously on the steering wheel. Beads of sweat covered his forehead. He had to find Preacher. Preacher could help.

Bobby Jack's worn brake pads made a metallic screech as he slowed to cross Dry Creek Bridge. He turned down a narrow lane that seemed to dead end into a branch of the creek. The stream, dried up by the lack of rain, left a profusion of slick rocks that layered the creek bottom. Each rock was worn smooth, with no sign of edges. Thousands of the limestone rocks lined the creek bed, making a road that could be used during dry weather. After heavy rains, the creek became a torrent of swift moving water that made it impassable.

Bobby Jack crossed the creek and stopped in front of a small, unpainted frame house. Preacher sat in the front yard, whittling. Foot-long curls of cedar shavings piled up around him. He leaned his rail-thin body back in the wooden chair and watched the red Ford truck pull into his yard.

He wasn't an actual preacher. His given name was Arthur Raymond Bess, but Bobby Jack doubted if anyone outside his family knew his real name. As a small boy, standing on a hickory stump imitating a local pastor, he had been given the name "Preacher."

Bobby Jack unfolded his 6'3" frame from the mud-splattered truck, ran his fingers through a mop of matted red hair, and walked over to where Preacher sat.

"Give me a swig," Bobby Jack said, pointing to a fruit jar filled with a dark golden liquid. Preacher spat on the ground and wiped the tobacco juice from his pockmarked face on the sleeve of his flannel shirt.

"Sure you can afford it?" Preacher asked. "It's my best stuff."

Bobby Jack grinned. Preacher filled a coffee cup and handed it to him. He raised the cup and drank deeply, the excess running down his chin. The sparkling moonshine burned like a hot poker. He swallowed with a gulp.

"People really buy this stuff?" Bobby Jack asked.

"Hell, yes," Preacher said. "Get $80 a gallon for it in Chicago. Dalton takes a load up there every couple of weeks. They buy all I can make."

Bobby Jack felt weak. His stomach growled. He hadn't eaten in a day, maybe two; he couldn't remember, but he wasn't hungry. He felt like he could throw up. He leaned against his truck and gave a heavy sigh.

"You look like shit," Preacher said, noticing his sunken cheeks. "How long have you been coming down?"

Bobby Jack took another long drink from the cup before he answered. "Since last night. I've had the shakes bad all day. I need a bump."

"Draino, battery acid. You gotta be crazy to shoot that stuff," Preacher said, shaking his head. Preacher reached in his shirt pocket, took out a joint, lit it, and handed it to Bobby Jack. "How much weight you lost? Forty or fifty pounds?"

"Ain't you got nothing else?" Bobby Jack asked, ignoring Preacher's questions.

"It's hard to get the stuff to make it since they passed all these damn laws."

"I need something more than this shit."

"I might have a little bit tomorrow," Preacher said.

Bobby Jack nodded. "Just a little hit will help."

"Take these and drink a lot of water," Preacher said, reaching into his shirt pocket and taking out three Xanax.

A longhaired dog of an unclear breed trotted up, wagging its tail. The dog nudged its nose against Bobby Jack's faded jeans. He squatted down, patted the dog's head, and rubbed his hand down its bony back. "Damn, Preacher, don't you ever feed this dog?"

Preacher removed the ever-present Camel from his mouth and stared at Bobby Jack. "Is that why you came here, to tell me how to take care of my damn animals?"

"No. I've got a way we can make some money, if you got a mind to," Bobby Jack explained.

Preacher laughed. "You back with your old lady again?" he asked with a smirk. "You always get ambitious when she's been nagging you about supporting her and that kid."

"Hell, no! I ain't never fooling with that bitch again."

"I've heard that tune before," Preacher said. "This ain't another one of them schemes like we got into cutting Josh McGregor's timber, is it?"

Bobby Jack shook his head, recalling one of his many ideas that didn't work out as he had planned. Josh McGregor lived in Nashville, but owned land in the Cove. Two years ago, they'd sawed timber on McGregor's land without him knowing it. It had been hard work. They had cut the timber and hauled it to the bottom of the mountain to be loaded. Before they could sell it, McGregor found out about it and sold it himself. They had done the work, and he had made the money. That seemed to be the way it went.

"Ain't you still working at the saw mill?"

Bobby Jack shook his head. "Timber here is about to play out," he said. He hated the drudgery of working the mill. He had to work off-chute, the hardest, dirtiest job at the sawmill. It didn't pay much. Even though he wore gloves, he always had splinters and blisters from the rough-sawn slabs.

Bobby Jack wanted to be somebody. He dreamed of driving a fancy car and living in a big house, but he knew it would never happen as long as he worked at a sawmill. He needed a good job, but jobs were hard to come by around here, especially if you didn't have an education.

Michael Clinton Oliver

He failed the third grade and the seventh. He'd missed a lot of school, which didn't help, but his major problem was that he never got the hang of reading. Not being able to read, and Miss Prichard, made everything difficult. She was his seventh-grade teacher, and for some reason, she never liked him.

Once, when the class had been doing fractions, Miss Prichard made him do a problem on the board. He copied down the problem, the chalk jerking unsteadily in his hand. The intricate lines trembled, ran together, and became almost unreadable.

Common denominators! For some reason, he forgot to find the common denominators before subtracting. Miss Prichard began berating him for making such a stupid mistake. She accused him of cheating on his homework and paddled him in front of the whole class. He never tried again in school. From that point on, teachers passed him just to get rid of a potential troublemaker. After the ninth grade, he dropped out, started hanging around Preacher's place, and working at the sawmill.

"Never knowed anybody to get rich working in a mill, did you, Preacher?" Bobby Jack asked.

"Don't know if I'd want to be rich," Preacher said. "Most folks I knowed that was rich ain't too happy, anyway."

Bobby Jack looked around Preacher's place. No one would ever accuse Preacher of being rich. His earthen yard had been worn so smooth by rain, only a few sprigs of grass could be found. Cigarette butts and beer cans littered the yard. Two large maple trees just beginning to bud provided the only sign of life.

A silver and blue Pontiac Sunbird, covered with a faded green tarp and speckled with chicken droppings, sat on blocks nearby. Preacher had talked about fixing it, or at least removing the parts and selling them, for over a year. It was one of many things Preacher had intended to do, but had postponed until a better time that never arrived.

"I know where we can buy a bunch of phosphorous and everything we need to make enough crank for everybody in the valley," Bobby Jack said. "Cheap."

He could tell by the way that Preacher's eyes twitched that he had gotten his attention. "Roger Thomas got busted, and his wife has his whole lab hidden in a shed behind her house. She's scared to death to try to sell it to somebody she don't know. Roger had a ton of stuff. Him and his old lady were separated, and he wasn't living there. That's the only reason the cops didn't find it."

Preacher took off his cap, revealing long strands of oily brown hair that only partly covered his balding dome. "So where do we come in?" Preacher asked.

"Martin's banging Lindsey, who is Roger's sister-in-law. She told him about it. She said we could get it for a couple grand," Bobby Jack said.

"Why don't we just steal it?"

"Roger's wife has two pit bulls in the pen where it's at."

"Where the hell are we going to get two grand?"

Bobby Jack shrugged his shoulders. He'd tried to think of everything since Martin told him about it, but so far, nothing seemed likely to get them that much money. He'd hoped Preacher would have a plan.

"Got a squirrel treed," Preacher said, hearing his dog barking in the woods nearby. "That dog can tree squirrels faster than you can shoot them out."

"Forget the damn dog," Bobby Jack said. "You got any ideas where we can get some money?"

"The only way you can get that kind of money round here is to steal it," Preacher said. Bobby Jack began to sweat again. He had known the truth all along, but hearing Preacher say it brought it closer to home.

Bobby Jack sat silently for a long time. "What about robbing the store in Sweetwater?" he asked, already uncertain that it was a good idea.

"How long you think it's going to take them to figure out who it is when a 6'3" redhead walks up to a cashier and asks for money?" Preacher asked. "You'll spend twenty years in prison for nothing."

Bobby Jack knew he was right. He shuddered at the thought of prison. He had been sent up for eighteen months for stealing a car. It had been one of those things that happened without really being thought through. He spotted a Corvette parked behind the Cracker Barrel in Manchester. A candy apple red convertible with wide raised-letter tires that made it appear to have been built for speed. He had always dreamed of a car like that. It had style.

He walked up as if he owned the vehicle. He popped the lock, and within minutes, he had exited the parking lot and was driving down the four-lane. Everywhere he went, heads turned. He felt great.

He was sitting at the Sonic having a cherry-limeade when a cop pulled in. Bobby Jack had been having such a good time that he didn't see the police cruiser until it stopped behind him. The officer got out of the car and drew his pistol. Bobby Jack surrendered meekly.

In court, he agreed to plead guilty to get a shorter sentence. He had been caught red-handed. Eighteen months was better than three to five years in prison. Still, that year and a half was hell. Damn, it made him smother to think about being locked up again.

"Only person I know with that kind of money is Ben Patton," Preacher said.

"He's your damn uncle!"

"He ain't no uncle of mine, that son-of-a-bitch."

"He's your mother's brother—"

"I don't give a damn who he is," Preacher shouted. "He ain't nothing to me."

When he spoke, the veins in his neck stood out like wires. His face was crimson and his voice high pitched and squeaky. "Mighty man! Big shot! The way he treated his own sister was a damn disgrace. I guess we was just too poor to fit in with the rich folks."

Bobby Jack didn't know what to say. He had been around Preacher long enough to know to let him finish letting off steam before interrupting him.

"My Mamma was a good woman," Preacher said. "I never knew my old man. Mamma raised me by herself. She did the best she could. She got diabetes and had to have her leg amputated. She lay there for months, dying, and the almighty Mr. Patton never once came to visit her."

Bobby Jack saw tears welling in Preacher's eyes and tried to look away. "I don't know," Bobby Jack said after a long pause. "If it wasn't Ben Patton—"

"He's a man, just like everybody else. You could bust in and tie him and his old lady up," Preacher said. "It shouldn't be no trouble. They're bound to have a lot of guns and jewelry. Everybody says he carries a lot of cash."

Bobby Jack knew Preacher would think of something. It all sounded so simple, but it was one thing to steal something when somebody wasn't looking, but could he pull a gun on somebody and rob them? Could he do it? he wondered.

"You might get a couple boys to go with you," Preacher said. "I'd go myself, but you know how my back is."

Bobby Jack tried to think. Martin would go, but he was just a kid. James had a broken foot; he wouldn't be of much use. He needed somebody to help in case of trouble.

"You think Dennis would go?"

"Dunno," Preacher said. "He needs money bad, with his Ma the shape she's in."

Bobby Jack liked the thought of having Dennis with him. If the chips were down, he knew he could count on his muscular friend for support.

"If a fellow needs money bad enough, he'll do about anything," Preacher continued.

It was coming together. He could see it working. There shouldn't be any problem. Ben Patton was an old man. Shouldn't be any problem at all.

"How about Rusty?" Preacher asked.

Bobby Jack shook his head. Like everybody else in the Cove, he disliked Rusty.

"He'd be a good one to have in case of trouble," Preacher said. "'Course, I don't expect you'll have any trouble."

Bobby Jack knew Preacher liked Rusty. If Preacher thought Rusty was all right, Bobby Jack was willing to take a chance.

"Yeah, why not?" he said. His time had come.

"You want to go with me to talk to Rusty?" Bobby Jack asked.

"Can't," Preacher said, a little sheepishly. "I'm going to church."

Bobby Jack looked surprised and decided Preacher was kidding him. "Yeah, right." he said.

Preacher got up from his chair. "Let's go inside," he said. "I want to show you something."

The floor joist sat on blocks. The blocks one side of the house had shifted, leaving the entire building looking rickety. The porch was weather-beaten and sunken in places. Heavy sheets of plastic concealed the windows, and a battered screen door safeguarded the entrance.

Preacher's house consisted of one main room and a back porch. The room smelled of stale smoke. A bed sat in a corner of the room, the sheets yellow with age. A small TV was situated in a chair near the bed. A kitchen table stood against the other wall, near a corroded sink filled with dirty dishes. A small kerosene heater warmed the house, although Bobby Jack thought it was still warm outside.

Faded yellow wallpaper adorned the bare walls. It was cracked and torn in places to reveal previous color schemes even more unsightly. Nails had been driven into the studs every few feet for Preacher to hang his clothes on. A light bulb dangled, uncovered, from the ceiling and provided a faint light.

Preacher went straight to a table beside his bed and picked up a picture. "That's Miss Mayes with my mama there," he said, pointing to one of the women in the picture. "She and Mama were best friends. She practically raised me after Mama died."

Bobby Jack took the picture and looked at it. The two women in the picture were young and obviously happy. They had their arms around each other, clowning for the camera. Something about the one on the left reminded him of Preacher. It must have been those near colorless grey eyes. He handed it back. Preacher stared at it a long time and put it back on the table.

"Miss Mayes came by this morning and asked me to go to the revival down at the church tonight. I couldn't turn her down after all she's done for me."

Bobby Jack looked at the picture again. He couldn't remember his mother, but he guessed she would look a lot like the women in the picture. His grandmother had told him she was a pretty woman. He wondered if she had ever been happy like them.

"I'm going to see Rusty and Dennis," Bobby Jack said, and he walked toward the door.

"Tell them we'll meet here Monday night at 8:00 PM," Preacher said. They walked out on the porch. The sky was darker than before. Clouds raced across the sky, partially obscuring the sun and casting an eerie shadow on the mountain. Lightning streaked across the western skyline.

"Get some religion for me, Preacher," Bobby Jack said, and walked out into the drizzling rain.

Chapter 2

It was an old stagecoach road that had been in general disuse since the end of the Civil War. In places, the path the road had taken was still evident underneath the rotting leaves and fallen tree limbs. Jake Patton strode at an easy pace along the trail. Heavy dew coated the grass, giving the appearance of a fresh rain. The temperature was cooler than he expected, and he turned up his collar to protect his face from the crisp air.

The sun peeped over the ridge and filtered through the trees, producing an iridescent collage of color on the surrounding mountainside. He stopped at Sycamore Falls to watch the clear water cascade over green, moss-coated rocks and disappear into the bubbly, white froth below.

He still had a couple miles to go to reach the Chimney. Though only four miles from the park entrance, it was isolated from the main trails, and few hikers in the Fiery Gizzard wilderness area ever found it. Jake had written most of *Arctic War* perched atop the fifty-foot-high rock formation that rose vertically from the surrounding valley.

He reached the Eagle's Nest, as the Chimney was officially known, about 7:00 AM. Ascending to the top was easy for an experienced climber, but there were a few difficult spots. The boots he wore were for hiking and not ideal for climbing. Though he had a rope in his backpack, he chose not to use it.

Once he reached the summit, he lay down on the cold rocks. The storm had passed and now the sky was powder blue. Wispy, white clouds hung vertically on the horizon. His father called them cow tails and said it was a sure sign of rain. Jake wasn't sure his father was right about the rain, but he wouldn't dare tell him he was wrong. Ben Patton had his own idea about things, and not even his youngest son could change his mind when it was made up.

Jake removed his notebook and began to write. A butterfly fluttered nearby, oblivious to the invasion of its habitat. It flew erratically, dipping, rising effortlessly in the wind, yet never seeming to reach its desired target.

Jake had been working on his second novel for more than a year with little success. He had to find the right words. He had the outline for the story. The Civil War served as a backdrop. Deserters from the Union army kidnap a young Rebel soldier's wife, and the husband searches valiantly to find her.

The heroine had a face. He had seen her in a dream. At least, he thought it was a dream. It had seemed so real.

He was staying at the Gulf Crest motel in Panama City. He had gone to the ocean to escape, something he did frequently in times of trouble. Lying on the beach in the sun with the warm wind blowing had always been relaxing. In the past, the rhythmic sound of waves crashing against the shoreline filled him with peace. This time, it seemed to yield little in the way of helping him unwind. It was the weekend of Shelby's wedding. He didn't want to be anywhere near Booneville that day, but being four hundred miles away hadn't made it any easier.

The apparition, if that is what it was, had come to him that night in Panama City. It wasn't Shelby. It didn't look like her, but he had a strange sense that the vision before him was somehow connected to her. She wore a flowing wedding dress and walked back and forth in the antebellum mansion, pleading for his help, looking out the window, chanting frantically.

I don't see the fish and fowl.
The killer whale or spotted owl
I don't see the bright blue sea,
The sparkling brook, or Redwood tree.

Out of the Darkness

When she left, he got out of bed and wrote down everything he could remember about her, including what she said. He had to make her the main character in his next book. She'd seared herself into his conscious, and he couldn't let her go.

He had the story in his mind, but it didn't flow. He had rewritten the opening scene dozens of times. It never seemed right. Some days, he wrote several pages, and after rereading it, tore it up and threw it all away. At other times, one or two sentences seemed to be a good day. He wanted it to be perfect, but it never was. Was he destined to be one of those one-hit wonders? A friend once said that everyone has one book in them. The really good writers could summon more out of the depths of their psyche.

Today, the words seemed to gush forth without effort. Before he realized it, the sun was high in the morning sky, warming his back. He almost didn't hear it. He was deep in thought and didn't hear the crashing noise until it was close. He stood and looked toward the sound. At first, he couldn't see anything. Then he spotted her, thrashing through the bushes, falling down, getting up, and running again.

"What's wrong?" Jake shouted.

She continued to stumble along before she realized someone was calling her. She stopped and looked around.

"Up here," Jake yelled waving his arms back and forth.

"Help me," she screamed.

Jake grabbed his rope, tied it to a nearby rock, and rappelled down the side. By the time he reached the bottom, she was there. "Are you all right?" he asked, noticing the cuts and scratches on her face and legs.

"I'm okay. My boyfriend fell off a bluff," she replied, regaining her composure.

"How bad is he hurt?"

"He's got a broke leg. He's bleeding some. I don't know. Please help me!"

Jake gave her a drink from his canteen. "Where did it happen?"

"A high point—in that direction," she said, pointing to the west.

"Raven's Point?"

She shrugged her shoulders and took a deep breath. "I don't know. It was our first time here. I'm from Mississippi. We both go to the University of the South."

Partin's Peak and Raven's Point were both in the direction she pointed, but were several miles apart. Time might be crucial if the boy was hurt badly.

"Was he an experienced climber?"

She nodded. "He said he had done a lot of climbing."

"It must be Raven's Point," Jake said, thinking an experienced climber would have little trouble scaling Partin's Peak.

"Let me take a look at that cut," Jake said, examining the gash above her left eye, which was oozing blood. He eased her blonde hair back from her face. She looked to be about eighteen, thin, but well built. Something about her reminded him of Shelby. He stopped the bleeding and placed a Band-Aid over the cut.

"Can you make it back to where he is?" Jake asked.

"Yes," she said. "Please hurry!"

"It's uphill and rough," Jake said, trying to discourage her.

"I'll make it," she replied.

Time was important. Jake walked fast, and the girl had trouble keeping up. "What's your name?" he asked when he stopped to let her rest.

"Allison," she said. "Allison Mitchell."

"Allison, the trail gets pretty steep the rest of the way. Why don't you stay here and rest while I go find your boyfriend?" Jake said. She appeared near exhaustion.

She shook her head. "I'll keep up."

The perimeter trail was an easier route to Raven's Point, but it took at least an hour longer. Jake plodded along, looking for gullies to take him to higher ground. Allison trailed some distance behind.

"Dale's not exactly my boyfriend," she said when Jake stopped to help her up a steep, slick slope. "We have a class together and have— Hey, I remember that," she said, pointing to an outcropping of rocks on the bluff above.

"Which direction is he from there?"

"Just to the left of that point—maybe a couple hundred yards."

They hiked as fast as possible, but walking was difficult. The underbrush was thick, and the terrain was beginning to rise sharply. Hundreds of large boulders and jagged rocks dotted the landscape.

"There he is!" Jake shouted.

The boy was lying on his back. His leg was at an awkward angle, obviously broken just below the knee. Dried blood had clotted around the protruding bone.

"Is he okay?" Allison asked, kneeling beside Jake as he examined the young man.

"He's breathing. His pulse is weak. When did this happen?"

"Yesterday afternoon."

"You mean he's been here all night?"

"It was almost dark when he fell. I didn't have a light and didn't want to go off in the dark by myself. I tried to keep him warm and stop the bleeding. I didn't know anything else to do but pray he'd be okay. I yelled and screamed, but no one heard me."

"You probably saved his life by getting the bleeding stopped," Jake said, looking at the makeshift bandage tied around the boy's leg.

"I started looking for help when the sun came up."

Jake shielded his eyes from the sun and surveyed the bluff. "He needs a doctor soon," Jake said. The bluffs were steep, but retracing his steps to the ranger station along the trail would be time consuming. It would take two hours, at least.

"The shortest way out of here is straight up," Jake said, taking off his shirt.

"What if you fall and—"

"I'm not going to fall, but if something did happen, go straight that way," he said, pointing west. In about a mile, you

15

will come to a small stream. Follow it downstream, and you will come to the perimeter trail. Once you find it, you can follow it to the ranger station."

"Please be careful."

Jake handed her his sweatshirt. "Try to keep him warm. I'll be back soon."

He made his way to the bluff and methodically began his ascent. The first thirty feet were easy. The route he had chosen had only one difficult spot. He didn't like heights, though he had scaled bluffs higher than this many times.

"That's where Dale fell," Allison shouted as he reached the difficult part of the climb.

He held his 200 lbs. with his left arm and foot and began to reach with his right to find a crack or ledge to hold. His left hand and foot hugged the rocks. He reached farther and farther. Nothing! He moved his weight back to his left side.

To get any higher, he was going to swing from one handhold to another like a kid on a jungle gym. He wouldn't be able to use his feet to help. The sharp crevice gouged his hand. Sweat dripped in his eyes, causing him to wince.

He looked down. Allison was pacing back and forth. They both knew what a fall from here meant. He gripped the crevice with his right hand and dried his left on his jeans. Re-gripping with his left hand, he swung hard toward the ledge above. His right hand latched to the edge. He dangled precariously above a bed of jagged boulders. The outcropping he was holding was too small to accommodate his left hand, which was useless against the slick face of the bluff. His feet clawed at the cliff, blindly searching for a foothold. He felt his grip slipping. He saw it—a tiny crevice near his right foot. He jammed his toe into the crack and pushed up, relieving some of the pressure on his right arm. He transferred his left hand to the ledge, and his right hand found a more secure hold.

"Are you okay?"

"Piece of cake," Jake yelled between deep breaths.

Out of the Darkness

When he reached the top, he waved at Allison. She looked tiny, kneeling beside her boyfriend. Jake admired her for her determination. He wasn't sure the boy would make it. He was severely injured. Ray Marcrom lived less than a mile away. He could call for help from there. Maybe it wouldn't be too late. Jake waved one last time. "I'll be back," he yelled, and took off running.

Chapter 3

Bobby Jack left Preacher's and drove down the narrow gravel road. He passed his brother's house. Neil's two kids were jumping on a trampoline. They waved as he passed, and he blew the horn and waved back. He drove on until he came to a fork in the road. He parked his truck on the side of the road and got out.

The old house that had once stood there had burned to the ground soon after Mr. Furness died. When Bobby Jack was a small boy—seven, maybe eight, his family lived just up the road from the Furness place. Mr. Furness had a very strong accent and was difficult to understand, but he always had a Butterfinger candy bar in his pocket to give Bobby Jack.

The fields where Mr. Furness had taken so much care to plant clover and timothy were now barren pastures. Three scrawny horses nibbled at the few sprigs of grass that grew here and there. The horses were hedged in by a grown up fencerows that hid any wire that might have at one time been there. It wasn't like that when Mr. Furness was alive.

Bobby Jack stared at the old barn, which had rotted and fallen in on itself. It tilted to the left in an awkward, deformed angle. The front of the barn remained upright in a futile effort to maintain its outward appearance. The rest of the barn was a pile of rusty tin and rotten lumber. It was all that was left of what had at one time been a sturdy structure.

Bobby Jack walked through the rain-slick grass to get a closer look. He pulled open the door and peered into the darkness. Gourds hung on a string inside the hallway. Mr. Furness had painted them to make birdhouses. Several lay crumbled and broken on the floor.

The ladder was still on the wall, just as it had been when Bobby Jack had slipped in and played there as a kid. Unlike the rest of the wood, it had been protected from the rain and still looked sturdy. He wanted to climb up to the hayloft once more, but the fallen timbers had sealed it off from the rest of the barn.

The door to the corncrib loomed straight ahead. As a kid, he had been afraid to open it. His older brothers told him that Mr. Furness had been a guard in a Nazi prisoner of war camp and that Mrs. Furness had been a nurse there. She had been driven insane by the awful medical experiments she had done to Jews and other prisoners.

The crib door always had a padlock on it. According to Bobby Jack's brothers, she was so crazy that Mr. Furness had to lock her in the crib to keep her from killing someone else.

Once, he had climbed up on some crates and tried to look through the cracks to see inside the crib. He had strained to get high enough. As he pressed his eye against the crack, he saw it, right in front of him—an old dilapidated wheelchair. He could only see one wheel, but it was there just as his brothers had told him. He heard a noise. The crates began to wobble, and he fell to the ground. He scurried out of the barn without looking back.

Now the door drew him to it. He had to find out what was inside. He undid the latch and opened the door of the corncrib. Its hinges creaked in dissent. He took a deep breath and stared into the darkness. Something in the back of the crib attracted his attention. It looked like someone's head. He squeezed in, past fallen timbers, until he could better make out the object's shape. He could see the old wheelchair, its back turned to him. Above the back of the wheelchair, there was an outline of a head. He saw the shape plainly now in the little light that served as a backdrop. He jumped back several feet. His heart beat wildly. His legs felt wobbly, and he leaned against the crib door for support. Could Mrs. Furness have been left inside and died right there in her chair? Surely, someone would have found her.

Some big farmer from Booneville had bought the place after Mr. Furness died. It was doubtful that he had ever been in here. Probably no one had been in there since Mr. Furness.

He tried to take another deep breath. Whatever it was, he was going to find out. He crawled back inside, grasped hold of the wheelchair, and pulled. It was stuck. He twisted it back and forth, attempting to free it from the timbers. He jerked harder. Without warning, it broke loose. The head tumbled off. It fell straight toward him. Bobby Jack screamed. The gourd fell on the floor and exploded into hundreds of pieces. Bobby Jack looked around to make sure no one else had seen what had happened. "A damn gourd," he muttered to himself.

Two boxes sat on top of each other in the seat of the dust-covered wheelchair. The gourd had been sitting on the top box. In the darkness, he couldn't tell what was in the boxes. He was sure they belonged to Mr. Furness, so he may as well take them.

He put the boxes in the bed of his truck. They smelled musty. He would open them later. Bobby Jack got back in his truck and sat there for a while. His heart was still beating rapidly. Things sure had changed.

He drove past the church and turned down a one-lane road running beside the creek. He crossed the creek and pulled into the driveway of a small, white house. The structure was old, but freshly painted. The tin roof looked new and black shutters hung evenly on each side of the windows. Firewood was stacked neatly on the concrete porch, and a plume of gray smoke drifted from the chimney.

Dennis Brock opened the screen door and walked out on the porch, drinking a can of Budweiser. His large, beefy hands wrapped around the can as if it were a toy. A mop of black, curly hair, thick enough to impede any brush, fell down on his bull-like neck. His round face showed signs of several days' growth of beard. Light brown eyes looked out at the world through perpetually sleepy eyelids.

Dennis stood only five feet eight inches tall, but he had been a good athlete. He had played third base on the team that won the thirteen-year-old state tournament. The high school coach had wanted him to come out for baseball, but he had never cared much for school and quit as soon as he was old enough. He had drifted from job to job, but always found work. Before his mom got sick, he hadn't needed a lot. He liked to coon hunt, and he had a blue tic hound that was as good as any dog in the Cove, better than most, in his opinion. Buckshot would never chase a fox or deer like some of the other dogs, and she always stayed at the tree until he got there.

He liked to hunt with his friends. Sometimes they would stay out all night. They would turn the dogs loose, build a big fire, sit around it, drink Preacher's moonshine, and smoke a few joints. He couldn't imagine anything he enjoyed more than getting high and gazing at the stars.

He worked on cars to make a little extra money. He had no formal training, but he was a good mechanic. He also dug some ginseng. The roots could be sold for a good price, but it was getting harder and harder to find. Money was scarce, but he made the best of his situation. He always had. His mama always taught him to do his best and not be anxious about the outcome, but he was a worrier. He guessed he got that from his father.

His father Henry had died two years ago, and now his mother was ill. She had spells when she couldn't remember things. They didn't have insurance, so she couldn't afford visits to the doctor. She needed to be in a nursing home, where someone could care for her.

Henry had suffered from black lung for several years, and that had drained their meager savings. Medical bills piled up, and they were more than Dennis could ever hope to pay, especially without a regular job.

He'd had a regular job with Tyson, but had failed a mandatory drug test. He had started using crank about a year and a half ago with Bobby Jack. Before that, he had never used anything stronger than pot. After the first time, he was hooked. He smoked it, snorted it, and shot it up every chance he got.

He had always been a big man, but going for days at a time without sleep or food had had a drastic effect on his body. He lost nearly eighty pounds in six months. He was constantly paranoid. He carried a gun with him at all times and had threatened to use it more than once. He still had scars on his arms from picking at the bugs he imagined were crawling beneath his skin.

He had been clean for a while now. His mother had been so ill that he'd had to straighten up to take care of her. His sister was too busy with her life to help, so it was left up to him. He was clean, but he still got the shakes. He couldn't even smoke a cigarette because it reminded him of getting high.

"Whatcha know good?" Dennis hollered at Bobby Jack as he got out of the truck. Dennis had always liked Bobby Jack; many people didn't, but you just had to know how to take him.

Dennis picked up a chair from the porch and carried it with him to the yard, where he turned it around and sat in it backwards. Bobby Jack walked unhurriedly to the porch and sat down, deliberately, like he did everything, took out his knife and began to whittle on the edge of the 4 x 4 post.

"How ya been?" Bobby Jack asked.

"Fair," Dennis said, sounding insincere. "How 'bout you?"

"If I can get the money to pay my fine, I can get my license back."

"You feeling okay?"

"Not good. I got the shakes really bad."

"You look like shit."

"I feel like it, too," Bobby Jack said. "You got anything?"

"Naw, I ain't had a hit in six months."

"I've been out a couple days. Got drunk at a party the other night, but it didn't help none."

"It never does. Hell, I can't drink nothing stronger than this," Dennis said, pointing at the beer can, "or I will go crazy."

"You've been clean six months?"

"Yeah."

"Don't you crave it?"

"I'd give my right arm for a lick right now!"

"Me too!" Bobby Jack said. "I got an idea how we can get all we want."

Dennis looked at him suspiciously. "Did you win the lottery?"

Bobby Jack laid out his plan. He could tell right away that Dennis didn't like the idea.

"Why the hell does it have to be Ben Patton?" Dennis mumbled in a voice too quiet for a man his size. "He was a real good friend of my pa's and—"

Bobby Jack interrupted, "'Cause he is the only one around here with that kind of cash. Everyone says he always carries a wad of money."

Dennis shook his head and muttered, "I ain't never done nothing like that."

"Nobody is going to get hurt," Bobby Jack assured him.

Dennis sat for a long time, shaking his head. Finally, he looked up.

"Who else is in on it?" he asked.

"Preacher knows, and I am going to get Martin and Rusty to go with us," Bobby Jack answered hesitantly.

"I don't like Rusty."

"I know," Bobby Jack agreed, "but we may need him if things get tough."

"Rusty is odd as hell."

"Just 'cause he's a Yankee. He ain't bad once you get to know him."

"Why the hell do we need Martin? He's just a kid."

"He knows how to make the stuff better than anyone. We'll need him when we get the money, so we might as well get him in on it now."

The sound of his mother's voice startled Dennis. "Dennis, you and Henry better get in here. It's time to eat supper."

"Yes, Ma. We're coming, right now," Dennis said, shaking his head. "She ain't always like that. Just here lately, it seems to be a little worse," he said, trying to explain to Bobby Jack.

Out of the Darkness

Bobby Jack nodded, a little embarrassed.

"I just don't know. If only it wasn't Ben Patton," Dennis said, recalling all the stories his father had told him about Ben. Henry had always had tremendous respect for Ben. He had always said no one could shoot a rifle like Ben Patton. "Pa would kick my butt for just thinking about it if he was still alive."

But his pa wasn't there, and there wasn't anybody to take care of his mamma but him. Damn, he sure needed the money. Bobby Jack said nobody would get hurt.

"Henry, we need a fire; I'm getting a chill."

"We're coming, Mama."

"Well, are you in or out?"

"I got a lot of responsibilities with Ma and all."

"You got a lot of debt, too."

Bobby Jack had no idea just how much doctor debt he had. He'd like to just get high and forget it. He sighed wearily. "When you gonna do it?"

"Be at Preacher's Monday night, 'bout dark."

Dennis nodded. The wind began to pick up. He walked back on the porch. Clouds were banking in the west; looked like a thunderstorm tonight.

Chapter 4

Preacher waited until it was almost time for the service to start before pulling into the church parking lot. The church looked much as it always had—a small, shabby, white frame building with a tin roof and tall, narrow windows. A few people were still hanging around outside. Men in blue jeans and flannel shirts smoked unfiltered cigarettes and talked about the weather. Young boys wearing blue jeans and tee shirts stood around, imitating the grown-ups.

Preacher thought about waiting until they went in. What the hell. They'd seen him, anyway. He walked toward the door and into the church. Several people turned to look, but no one spoke to him.

The inside looked much as he remembered. The pot-bellied stove that once overheated the one-room building was gone, replaced by wall heaters. The floor was still rough and uneven. The old, slatted pews had been replaced with some a little more comfortable, though they weren't padded.

A large picture was the focal point on the wall behind the pulpit. Jesus was kneeling, his elbows resting on a great rock. He stared toward heaven, apparently praying for deliverance from the cross. Beams of light radiated from his weathered face. He looked sad, as if the weight of the world was upon his shoulders. In a way, it was. Preacher never understood why Jesus had to die to save mankind. It just didn't make good sense.

He sat down near the back. Miss Mayes, a perky, gray-headed lady, smiled when she saw him come in. The service hadn't started, and she walked back to where he was, her black polka-dotted dress beaming like hundreds of tiny lights.

"Glad you came, Arthur," she said. "I've been praying for you."

"Thank you, ma'am," Preacher mumbled as he stood to shake her hand.

Miss Mayes grabbed the arm of a man dressed in a dark grey suit as he walked by. "Reverend Simmons, I'd like you to meet someone. This is Arthur Bess. His mother and I were best friends. She attended this church when Brother Ferrell was the pastor here."

"Nice to have you here, Arthur," the pastor replied. "I hope you will come and worship with us more often."

Preacher nodded. The pastor excused himself and made his way to the front of the church. Several other members of the congregation came by, shook his hand, and welcomed him. He couldn't help but wonder what they really thought about him.

"Do you want to sit up front with me and Doris?" Miss Mayes asked.

"No, ma'am. I'll just sit back here," Preacher said, wishing he could sit in the back row, which had been taken by a group of teenagers.

"I'll just sit back here, too," she said, and sat down.

"Praise the Lord," the pastor shouted. He stood behind the pulpit and surveyed the congregation. "It's great to see all you folk out tonight. God's going to do a miracle right here in this cove." A cacophony of amens and hallelujahs followed. "Before Brother Wilkinson brings us the message, we want to go to the Lord in prayer and ask his blessing on tonight's service. Are there any requests?"

At the front of the church, a woman Preacher didn't recognize got to her feet and said, "Miss Annie Thomas is in the hospital and not doing too well. Wish everyone would remember her in your prayers."

Mrs. Edna Bean, a tiny lady that lived just up the road from Preacher, stood. "Wish you'd remember Ed Caldwell's family. Ed died of cancer last week, and his family is taking it mighty hard. They got a lot of medical bills, too."

"The Lord will provide," the pastor said. "Is there anyone else?"

"Albert Parker," several people said at once.

"Yes, let's be sure to remember Brother Parker," the pastor said. "I visited with him and Jean this past week, and he is not doing well. We especially want to remember those that are sin sick. There are so many in our midst that are lost and on their way to a devil's hell."

Preacher felt like people were looking at him. He was already beginning to sweat. Damn. He wished he hadn't come, but he couldn't get up and leave. The clock on the wall behind him kept ticking louder and louder. Every second punctuated with a harsh click.

"Tick!"
"Tick!"
"Tick!"

"Let us pray," the pastor continued, and began to lead the congregation in a rambling prayer. Everyone was praying aloud at the same time, and Preacher was unable to follow even the pastor's prayer.

"Tick!"
"Tick!"
"Tick!"

After the prayer ended, Orin Roberts led them in a couple congregational hymns. The first one seemed vaguely familiar. Orin was off-key, and the piano was still out of tune, but no one seemed to notice.

Preacher was taken aback by the words to the second song. It was his mother's favorite song. She sang it to him many times when he was just a child.

Alas! And did my savior bleed? And did my sovereign die?
Would he devote that sacred head for such a worm as I?
He loves me, he loves, he loves me this I know.
He gave himself to die for me because he loved me so.

He and Ed Darling had got into a fight over that song when they were kids. Ed had made fun of Preacher singing the "such a worm as I" part.

"What kind of damn worm are you, Arthur?" he had sneered. "A grub worm?"

Even though Ed was four years older and bigger, Preacher had taken a punch at him, not so much for calling him a worm, but for making fun of his mamma's song. Ed bloodied Preacher's nose before Brother Ferrell broke up the fight.

Brother Ferrell had taken a white handkerchief out of his pocket and wiped the blood off Preacher's nose and lip. They sat down on a hickory stump. It was fall, and hickory nuts littered the ground. A squirrel ran out on a limb carrying a nut and jumped from one tree to the next. "Let me take a look at that," Brother Ferrell said after the bleeding stopped. "I believe you are going to live."

Preacher was still mad, but he grinned. "Ed Darling won't be living if he makes fun of my mama again."

"Is that what caused all the ruckus?" Brother Ferrell asked, taking off his hat to reveal a completely bald head, except for a few tufts of gray hair around his ears.

Preacher explained what had happened. Brother Ferrell put his arm around Preacher's shoulders. "You let me take care of Ed," he said. "I don't want to see you fighting. Your mamma wouldn't like it, either." Preacher didn't know what Brother Ferrell said to Ed, but he never goaded him again.

Preacher was jolted back to reality. The offering plates were being passed down the isle. He dug in his pocket, pulled out a wadded dollar, and dropped it in the plate. Churches were always begging for money.

The offering was carried back to the front and placed on the altar. "Glory to God," the pastor said.

He introduced Brother Wilkinson, the guest evangelist who greeted the congregation. He had silver hair, combed straight back. "If everyone will stand for the reading of God's word," he said with a smug look on his face.

Out of the Darkness

Preacher was relieved to stand. The benches were hard, and his back ached, but it always did. Ever since he went down in that chopper in Vietnam, he couldn't sit long without his back stiffening. Guess he was lucky to be alive, though.

Ten men in his platoon had been on a scouting mission near Khe Sanh when the Viet Cong ambushed them. Preacher heard the sound of automatic weapons coming from the curtain of green undergrowth to his left. He fired his automatic weapon blindly as he ran through the sloppy gray ooze. Bullets hissed all around. Preacher saw their sergeant, Billy Self, a big, raw-boned farm boy from Hueytown, Alabama take three or four rounds in the chest. Preacher didn't stop to see if he was alive. Corporal Jay Arp tried to drag the NCO to cover, but he was hit in the back and legs. They lost two more men in a running gun battle along a rice paddy. The radioman, Gene Watson, called for a helicopter to pick them up. They hunkered down behind thick elephant grass until they heard the familiar "whomp, whomp, whomp" of a helicopter. The Huey came in low, trying to keep away from the gunfire until the last second. It hovered like an angry green bumblebee, its sixty-caliber machine gun raking the jungle with a barrage of bullets. The Huey launched rockets from underneath its fuselage at the tree line in a desperate attempt to cover the retreating men. When Preacher and the others reached the clearing where the chopper was trying to land, they were met with heavy gunfire. They lobbed a few grenades toward the wooded area from where the shots were coming and clambered aboard the chopper, firing toward the grove of trees. It was hot, and the fully loaded chopper struggled to get off the ground. A burst of ground fire tore into the rear rotor, sending the helicopter into a wild spin. The pilot grappled with the controls before stabilizing the craft.

"Get up! Get up!" the pilot shouted, trying to will the chopper above the trees. The helicopter struggled and groaned. For a while, it looked like they were going to make it. They were getting close to their own lines when the helicopter gave a loud coughing sound and began to sputter.

"We're going down!" the pilot yelled as he tried to make it to an open field. One of the struts caught a limb and sent the chopper crashing to the ground, where it burst into flames.

Mike Rhomeir from Oklahoma had been sitting next to him when the chopper hit the trees; the occupants were tossed around the inside like popcorn. Almost in slow motion, they tumbled to the ground, the limbs of the trees snapping and cracking, unable to withstand the weight of the wreckage. Preacher didn't remember hitting the ground. He awoke to the heat of flames licking at his face. His leg was caught in the tangled debris. The heat singed his face and hair. Preacher had pulled and twisted, and somehow managed to free himself. Mike was screaming for help. Preacher tried to reach him, but the flames were too hot. He was trying to find someone to help him when the fuel tanks erupted, hurling Preacher to the ground. His face, hands, and arms were burned, but he was alive. He would never forget the roar of the flames and the screams of the men.

"If you will turn to the fifth chapter of the Gospel of Matthew, beginning at verse seven."

Blessed are the merciful, for they shall obtain mercy.
Blessed are the pure in heart, for they shall see God.
Blessed are the peacemakers, for they shall be called the children of God.

Mercy. Preacher didn't know much about mercy. When he thought about how Mike and the others had suffered, he didn't see much of God's mercy. *If he was such a loving creator, why did he allow bad things to happen to good people?* His mother had suffered terribly with cancer before she died and left him alone in the world. What good had her religion done her?

The evangelist's voice rose and fell for emphasis. *Brother Ferrell had never yelled like that.* Preacher was lost in his own thoughts. *Why did my mother have to die? If she were here, things would be better.*

Out of the Darkness

"If everyone would please stand," the evangelist said after a lengthy sermon. The congregation rose in unison.

"We are going to sing a song of invitation," he continued. "Don't be ashamed to come to this altar. It's a place to find healing. It's a place to find hope and peace." The piano player started playing softly.

"It's at the foot of the cross where you can find rest. Jesus came and bled and died that each of us could have forgiveness for our sins, no matter how bad a sinner we have been."

Preacher was sure the speaker was talking directly to him. He fidgeted, shifting his weight from foot to foot. He gripped the pew in front of him tightly, never daring to raise his head and make eye contact with anyone.

They sang several verses of invitation. Several people went to the altar to pray. When the invitation was given for others to come and pray with those around the altar, Preacher slipped out of the church and into the darkness.

Chapter 5

"We're going to a party at Jerome's house tonight," Rusty said, slamming the door of the trailer behind him. He opened the refrigerator and grabbed a beer. "Damn thing ain't working right again," he complained, rubbing his hand across the can, which was warmer than he liked.

"Nicole's sick," Shelby began to protest, but he had already left the room, not waiting to hear her reply. She followed him into the living room, where he sat on a brown, threadbare couch removing his cowboy boots.

"I've already talked to Jenny Meeks, and she's on her way over to baby-sit." Shelby didn't answer, but he could tell by the look on her face that she was unhappy. "I really want to go, baby," he pleaded, the way he always did when he wanted his way.

"But Nicole's sick, and I—"

"Quit whining and get dressed," Rusty yelled. He slammed the half-empty can on the table and walked away. Shelby knew better than to argue. She cleaned up the beer and went to the tiny bathroom to get ready.

She didn't recognize the person she saw in the mirror. Creases were beginning to adorn her once smooth complexion. The powder she brushed on was unable to stem the tide of time. Her once vibrant and bouncy blonde hair looked dull and listless. She ran her comb through it, dissatisfied at the result. She applied eye shadow to blue eyes that had at one time sparkled and danced, but now appeared listless. The happiness had faded, and the emptiness showed.

Rusty did a quick set of curls and came into the bathroom flexing his biceps. "Hurry up!" he shouted, "I don't want to be late."

She dressed quickly and went in to check on Nicole. "Mommy will be back soon," she whispered, pulling the cover around the four-year-old's neck and brushing back her dark hair. The child's face was flushed.

"Don't go, Mommy," Nicole pleaded as Shelby left the room.

Shelby went back and sat on the bed. "Mommy has to go somewhere with Daddy, but she will be back soon. Go to sleep. When you wake up, I'll fix you some pancakes." Nicole's brown eyes looked sad, but she nodded her head. Shelby kissed her and hurried from the room.

Jenny was waiting for her at the kitchen table. Shelby wrote the Dotsons' phone number on a torn envelope and attached it to the refrigerator with a "Home Sweet Home" magnet. "Our phones are out. They were supposed to come today and fix them. You can go next door to Miss Fannie's if you need to call us," Shelby said after giving some last minute instructions.

Rusty was waiting in the truck when she got there, drumming his fingers impatiently on the steering wheel.

"Nicole is pretty sick," Shelby said. "I don't want to be gone long."

"We won't stay too long. I just want to get out and relax."

"If she's not better tomorrow, I think we need to take her to the doctor."

"There goes more money."

"She's got a high fever—"

"You take her. You know how much I hate doctor's offices."

"Okay," Shelby said, shrugging her shoulders and turning to stare out the window at the mountains in the distance.

"There's supposed to be a lot of people at the party tonight." The rest of the short drive to the party was silent except for the sound of a country station on the radio.

Several cars were already parked in the Dotsons' driveway when they arrived. Rusty pulled into a field that had been converted into a parking lot. He killed the engine and strode to the front door. Shelby followed several steps behind.

Jerome and Debbie Dotson lived in a roomy, white frame house about halfway between Dry Creek Cove and Booneville. The house was old; its tin roof streaked with rust. The wooden porch had recently been repaired in several places. Shelby could smell the freshly sawed wood. The new boards offered a sense of cleanness to an otherwise dingy house.

Jerome met them at the door with a half-empty bottle of Jack Daniels in his hand. His thinning brown hair was uncombed, and he spoke slower than usual.

"Hey, gang," he said, holding open a weather-beaten storm door. "Y'all come on in and grab a drink." Rusty slapped Jerome on the back, and Shelby followed them into the dimly lit room. The music was blaring.

A strobe light was flashing, and several couples were dancing on a newly carpeted floor. *I guess it's dancing,* Shelby thought, though it appeared to be a cross between a waltz and the animated grope of lovers.

Rusty went straight to the bar, a wide board sitting on two barrels. "What's going on?" Rusty asked a boy slowly filling a plastic cup from one of the kegs.

"Party time," the boy shouted over the music and staggered away, a little unsteady. Shelby didn't know him, but she was sure he wasn't over sixteen.

Rusty filled a cup, raked the head off with his hand, took a long drink, and refilled it. "Want some beer?" he asked, noticing Shelby. She grabbed a clear plastic cup without answering and filled it half-full. She took a sip and made a face. She had never learned to like the pungent taste, and this seemed worse than most.

Rusty swaggered over to a group of men huddled around a card table. His jeans appeared to be an extension of his skin. He was short and cocky. When they first met, that confidence had been an attraction, but it was all a façade, like veneer covering a scarred floor. He was two different people, the one he pretended to be, and the one he really was. It was one of the many things about him she hated.

Rusty spied Preacher Bess and made his way to the corner of the room where Preacher was sitting. She couldn't understand why Rusty liked Preacher. He always gave her the creeps. She didn't like Rusty hanging out with him, but there wasn't much she could do.

Left alone to fend for herself, Shelby looked for a familiar face. It seemed she had stood alone all her life, listening to the sound of laughter that always drifted out of her reach. Why? Why was she different?

Looking around the room, she spotted Carrie Johnson sitting on a couch. She eased her way through the crowd and sat down. Carrie tossed her curly red hair out of her eyes and smiled. She wasn't pretty, though something about her tomboy looks made her attractive. Carrie wore a light khaki skirt that slid way above her bony knees. Carrie and Shelby had been friends since grammar school. Soon they were engrossed in conversation and lost track of time. They had a unique ability to be able to pick up a conversation after months of absence as if they had never been apart.

Several people were lighting joints and passing them around. The distinct, sweet smell of marijuana drifted in the air. Someone passed a joint to Shelby. Not wanting to draw attention to herself, she took a short toke and passed it to Carrie.

"I'm pregnant, you know," Carrie said, giggling, and passed the joint to someone else. The music, the beer, and the marijuana in the air had the desired effect. Shelby began to relax. It had always been hard for her to loosen up, but for a brief time her problems began to fade away in a haze of smoke and explosion of music.

"How's things?" Carrie asked.

Shelby shrugged. "Like always."

"You don't have to put up with that," Carrie said. "I didn't."

"Little different when you have a kid," Shelby said, wishing she had Carrie's spunk.

"I guess I'll find out soon," she said, rubbing her stomach, though she was not beginning to show.

"Yeah, you'll see just how different it is," Shelby said.

"Guess who I saw at Wal-Mart?"

"No idea," Shelby said.

"No, you gotta guess."

"Elvis?"

"Be serious."

"Really, I have no idea," Shelby said.

"You once told me his kisses made you see stars," Carrie said, unable to stop giggling.

"You saw Jake?" Shelby asked. Carrie nodded her head still giggling. "Is he living here now?"

"That's what he told me," Carrie said. "He said he had moved back to stay."

"I knew he built a big house, but I thought he would be living in New York or somewhere after he hit it big," Shelby said.

"Did you read *Arctic War*?" Carrie asked. Shelby shook her head, remembering how mad Rusty had been at her for even mentioning it. "The girl in the story—I think her name was Cassie. Anyway, that was you."

Shelby laughed. "No way, you're crazy!"

"Oh, yeah. She was blonde, 5'7", blue eyes, and an artist. Sound like anybody we know?"

"I'd hardly say I am an artist," Shelby argued.

"I've seen your paintings."

"When did you become an art critic?"

"When did you become a doormat?" Carrie asked and instantly regretted she had said it. Shelby looked down. Carrie grabbed her arm. "Honey, I'm sorry I said that. It's just I hate to see you so unhappy. You were my best friend, and we haven't even talked in months."

Shelby sobbed. "I don't know how things got so mixed up. Rusty is so jealous. He doesn't want me talking to anybody."

"Damn it, Shelby. Why don't you leave him?"

"It's not that easy."

Gail Baxter and Jennifer Winstead came and sat next to them on the couch. After several minutes of idle conversation, several other people joined their group. Shelby wanted to hear more about Jake, but it was impossible to continue their conversation with so many people around.

Carrie stood and stretched. "I'm still hungry. You know how it is when you are eating for two." While she was gone, Shelby weaved between dancing couples in search of a restroom. As she reached the bathroom door, someone grabbed her by the arm. She turned to see the drunken, grinning face of Bobby Jack Morris.

"How about a dance, pretty woman?" he asked, pinning her against the wall with his arm.

"Take your hands off me or—"

"Or what? Your old man seemed pretty entertained with Laura out in the back yard," he said, pleased by her reaction. She pushed his arm away and marched back through the living room to the back yard.

Shelby opened the screen door and bounded down the steps. In the corner of the yard, she spotted Rusty and Laura Greer on a wooden picnic table. Laura's blouse was undone. Rusty's hands and mouth ravaged her exposed flesh.

"I'm going home!" Shelby shouted. "You stay here with your little whore!"

Rusty looked stunned. "Let me explain," he stammered. Shelby didn't stay to listen. She stormed back inside. Rusty didn't follow.

Shelby brushed by several people until she got a glimpse of Carrie. "Can you give me a ride? I need to check on Nicole."

"Sure," Carried replied, knowing there was more to it than that, but friend enough to wait until Shelby wanted to talk about it.

Shelby hurried to the bedroom and rummaged through the coats on the bed. She sensed someone standing behind her.

"Sorry about being a jerk and telling you what was going on out back," Bobby Jack stammered. "I just thought you should know. You deserve better."

Shelby nodded, snatched her coat, and rushed out of the house.

The ride home was quiet except for gravels pinging the underside of Carrie's Mustang. They hurled through the darkness on the curvy road. Carrie shifted gears like a racecar driver. She drove past Dry Creek Bridge and turned into Shelby's driveway.

"If you want to talk about it—" Carrie began, but stopped short of finishing.

Shelby nodded. "Right now, I just need to be by myself," she replied, sniffing to hold back tears.

Shelby paid Jenny and hurried to check on Nicole. She was fast asleep. Shelby got in bed, but she couldn't rest. She tried to watch TV, but her mind kept returning to the Dotsons' back yard. Rusty hadn't even tried to stop her from leaving.

The sound of Rusty's truck woke her from her restless slumber. She looked at the clock. It was almost 3:00 AM. Rusty stumbled through the trailer, cursing, knocking things over. Shelby edged to her side of the bed, hoping he would leave her alone.

"Why the hell did you leave the party?" he shouted. "It was just starting to get good."

"Nicole's asleep. Hold your voice down," Shelby said, trying to avoid a confrontation.

"Laura is a hell of a woman," he shouted, even louder than before. "She knows how to treat a man." The incident at the party had been just one of a long line of abuses. Catching him undressing Laura Greer shouldn't have been that much of a surprise.

Rusty jumped on the bed, grabbed her hair, and turned her over to face him. His breath smelled of strong whiskey, and he spit his words, cursing her for deserting him. He pinned her to the bed and kissed her roughly. She tasted her own blood. He forced his mouth against hers.

She struggled to make him quit, but he was too strong. She continued to fight, scratching his face, but the blows hit her from all angles. She tried to block the punches, but the pummeling continued unabated. Everything became fuzzy, and then came the sweet relief of darkness.

When she regained consciousness, Rusty was asleep. His thunderous snores vibrated the room. She slipped out of bed and made her way unsteadily to the bathroom. She quietly closed the door and turned on the light. Her face in the mirror surprised her. Her right eye was swollen, and her lip was split at the corner of her mouth. Her stomach hurt worse than ever before. She rubbed her frail hand across her injured face. Dried blood matted her long, blonde hair. The white cotton tee shirt she wore as a nightgown was stained a dark crimson.

She hobbled into the kitchen. "Damn him," she muttered. She went to a cabinet next to the refrigerator and got a pistol. The gun was almost too heavy to lift. She walked gingerly to the sink, reached underneath, and pulled out an old coffee can filled with sponges and scrubbing brushes. She dumped the contents of the can into the sink. Unable to straighten because of the pain in her side, she lay down on the floor and curled in a fetal position.

Why is God allowing this to happen to me? Why must I live in this hell? She was suffocating—trapped like an animal in a cage. She had seen lions and tigers at a local fair when she was a little girl. All the other kids had been excited to see the strange, exotic animals, but she kept noticing the bars that kept them confined in an artificial world, made to resemble their natural surroundings.

She was trapped like those animals, and like them, she had no hope of escape. If just once she could be free—but she knew she would never be free of him. She was just an actor in a drama that had already been written. The ending was a mere formality.

She was lonely. Rusty had isolated her from her friends and family. She was alone in a world where everyone else had companionship. It was like she was living someone else's nightmare, but the fog never lifted.

She had tried to talk to Rusty. At first, he tried to listen, but she could tell by the dull look in his blue eyes that he would never change. She was alone at home and alone in a crowd. His presence made her feel even more alone. She despised him, but there was no hope of escape. He would kill her if she tried to leave. She never doubted that for a moment.

He had been different from other boys she had known. He was rugged and defiant, the opposite of her in every way. It had been a magnetic attraction, but there had been a dark side.

The nickel-plated barrel of the .357 Magnum glistened in the pencil thin streaks of moonlight that cascaded through the open curtain into the darkened room. He had given her the gun and taught her to shoot it. He would probably be happy she had the courage to use it.

Tears chased tears down her face, cascading like waterfalls into the cut on her lip. The salt burned her bleeding lips, but she was oblivious to the brackish taste. Her lips quivered. She absently wiped her tears with her hair.

With trembling hands, she reached in the coffee can and pulled out the false bottom she had made out of tinfoil. Underneath was a picture. She looked at it and smiled for a moment. Someone had taken a picture of Jake Patton and her hiking in Savage Gulf. The faces in the picture were happy and carefree. Her head was leaning on Jake's shoulder, her blonde hair in stark contrast to his brown, nearly black, hair. He had both arms around her, holding her tight. His arms were muscular and tanned.

The picture had been taken on a bluff at Stone Door, a narrow passageway that led from the top of the mountain to the gorge below. She had been scared standing close to the edge, but when Jake held her, she knew she was safe. Jake had a way of making other people feel protected in his presence. She couldn't remember feeling secure since.

Jake had been her first love. The feeling never went away, no matter how hard she tried. She had given him her heart and soul, and he had broken her heart. She was devastated.

A friend had introduced them at school. Jake had been polite, but hadn't had much to say. Her first impression was that he was arrogant. A few weeks later, she saw him at a party, surrounded by a group of people. When she finally saw him alone, she summoned all her courage and began talking to him. They began dating that night.

He was tall, dark, and handsome, just like the prince in a fairy tale book. But, it was his dark, brown eyes that made her melt. He was an all-state quarterback on the football team and had been drafted in the late rounds by the St. Louis Cardinals in baseball. Shelby had attended all the games, worn his jacket with "Patton" on the back, and had been the envy of all the girls. She was in heaven. He was all she had ever dreamed about, but in the end, it was only a dream.

They dated for over a year, and he broke up with her. She never understood why. She thought it had something to do with his parents, but he wouldn't talk about it. He told her he wanted his ring back, and that had been it. She cried for days and never got over the pain. She met Rusty a few months later.

The break-up with Jake crushed her; being with Rusty made it all seem better. He was new in school, having just moved to Dry Creek Cove from Chicago. He was lonely and seemed to care about her. She needed to be held and told she was loved, and in the beginning, he had filled that need.

She had talked to Jake one time after she and Rusty started dating. It had been such a stupid thing and so uncharacteristic. She had always been faithful to Rusty, but she knew in her heart that she loved Jake.

Graduation night, Rusty left her to go drinking with his friends. She felt rejected. It was the biggest night of her life, and she wanted to be with Rusty, but he preferred to be out getting drunk. Someone invited her to go to a graduation party. She had gone to the party, but for most of the night, she sat on the couch feeling sorry for herself. Jake Patton had strolled up and started talking; it was the first time they had really talked since the break-up.

Jake offered to drive her home, and she had accepted with some hesitation. It hadn't turned out the way she imagined, although affairs of the heart seldom follow a prescribed script. They talked as if they had never been apart.

He drove down the dark country road toward her house. He twirled his fingers through her hair and told her how beautiful she looked. The back of his hand brushed her cheek, and her body began to quiver. Her heart pounded. She couldn't think. She kissed his hand and arm. He stopped in the middle of the road and kissed her softly. Her lips parted; they meshed as one. The windows were down, but the air was suddenly hot. She struggled to breathe. She felt tingles all over her body. Jake's kisses electrified her in a way Rusty's never did.

Jake drove to a spot on the Patton farm that overlooked Booneville. He kissed her neck tenderly. His tongue flicked her earlobe and moved down her neck. Chill bumps covered her entire body. His hand slipped under her shirt. She shuddered uncontrollably. His hands felt like burning coals against her soft flesh. They kissed deeply as he undressed her. The passion she felt that night was unlike any she had felt before or since. They made love underneath the stars; it was magical. She had hoped that night would never end.

It was her first time. She had planned to save herself for marriage, but she couldn't withstand her desire. She knew it wouldn't change things between them, but she didn't care. Lying next to Jake was something she had longed for.

Someone told Rusty she had been with Jake. He interrogated her about it the next day. She admitted Jake had given her a ride home, but denied anything else had taken place. She hated to lie. Her feelings for Rusty were different from those she had for Jake, but she feared being alone.

Though her parents protested, she married Rusty two weeks after graduation. A month later, she found out she was pregnant. She thought a child might change Rusty. Maybe it would keep him home and make him love her more. Instead, it only made things worse. He gave Nicole little attention, and when he got mad at her, he took it out on Shelby.

How had her life gotten so out control? What had happened? It seemed like yesterday that she was young and happy, but that was an eternity ago. How could someone say he love you one minute and beat you the next? How could the person you chose to spend your life with, who you thought loved you, have affair after affair? What had she done wrong?

When she married, she was full of romantic ideas. She wanted so much for him to love her. Even when he beat her, she begged him to forgive her for what she had done. She thought he would love her if she cooked better, cleaned house better, was better in bed, or lost weight. She tried everything, but no matter what she did, he told her she was ugly and worthless. He constantly berated her for being a lousy wife. The only person he cared about was himself.

Was he right? No matter what she did, she could never please him. She wasn't a competitor. She couldn't win against an unknown challenger. Someone would always be prettier, smarter, better at everything than she was.

Her index finger tightened around the trigger. She raised the gun and placed it against her temple. Her mind accelerated, rewinding, and fast-forwarding the existence that was her life.

She recalled the first time he hit her, four days after their wedding. He had given her a black eye. She tried to remember what she had done to make him mad. He hit her in the stomach too many times to count when she was pregnant. He was always slinging her across rooms and bouncing her off walls. No matter what he did, she begged him to forgive her. She was sure she had done something to deserve being hurt. It made her sick to think of the way she had allowed herself to be treated.

The longer they were married, the worse the beatings became. Broken noses, fractured ribs, and numerous cuts and bruises were almost monthly happenings. He always promised that it would never happen again. He cried and begged her to forgive him, and she always did. His promises were like letters written in the sand, the first wave made them almost unreadable and the second made it appear it was never there at all. She had been such a fool, making excuses for his behavior and telling people she had fallen down a flight of stairs or bumped into a door.

Control. That was the name of his game. He questioned her every time she went anywhere, wanting to know whom she had talked to and where she had been. She had to ask permission to go anywhere, even the grocery store. He inspected the mileage on her car to see if she drove farther than what she told him. Every move she made he checked. He accused her parents of trying to cause trouble because they were concerned about her welfare. At one time, he had removed the phones to keep them from calling.

She had thought about killing herself frequently during their four years of marriage. Dying would be better than to go on living the way she had. She didn't want it to end like last time. Two years earlier, she rammed her head through a plate glass window. She thought he would worry about her and realize that he loved her. They drove to two different emergency rooms because he hadn't wanted to wait in the first one.

The cut on her head required fifteen stitches to close. After returning home, he accused her of wanting to sleep with the doctor in the emergency room. He backhanded her, opening the cut on her already aching head.

This time, I'm going to do it, she thought. She rocked back and forth on the floor, like a baby in a cradle. She felt like screaming. Her muscles tensed. The hammer moved slowly back.

A barking dog broke the silence in the room. The gun flew out of her hand and bounded across the floor. "I can't do this to my family. Not yet," she whispered. "What would happen to Nicole?"

She crawled to where the pistol lay and cradled it to her breast. "I can't do anything right," she cried. "Even kill myself!" She picked herself up from the floor, wrapped the gun in some old rags, and placed it with care in the drawer where she could find it when she needed it. She knew she would need it, she just didn't know when.

Chapter 6

The final amen sounded, and the congregation began to busy themselves catching up on the latest gossip. The pastor, wearing a suit and tie, not a formal robe, made his way to the back of the sanctuary to shake hands with the people. A small, balding man in his early fifties, he had moved to the valley six years earlier from the mid-west and was firmly established in his position as pastor and community leader. His unassuming, reserved manner belied a quiet confidence that fit the stereotype members of his church had of what a minister should be.

He also possessed the expertise needed to design and build what most people considered the "most attractive" place of worship in the area. With the help of everyone in the congregation that could drive a nail, saw a plank, carry water, or provide encouragement, they built the church from the ground up. Plush by country standards, the sanctuary possessed a hint of modern architecture, but overall, it was clearly orthodox. The stained glass windows were the church's most attractive features, even if its huge steeple was its most noticeable one.

The building was located in a serene valley surrounded by picturesque mountains. Autumn was beautiful with its dazzling array of red and gold, and in the wintertime, the snow clung to the trees, painting everything a radiant white, but in springtime, everything woke from its slumber to burst forth with a spectrum of color. The trees were just beginning to show their emerald foliage. After a winter of snow and drab hue, the mountain had suddenly come to life with color. Dogwood trees were in full bloom, coating the countryside with splashes of brilliant white against the green. Redbud trees, which seldom bloomed so beautifully because of the late frost, had been spared this year and added a radiant tint to the landscape.

The crowd continued to mingle outside the church, long after their dismissal, enjoying the mild spring day. Services had lasted longer than usual, but no one seemed to be in any hurry to get home.

The pastor walked out into the bright sunshine. "I enjoyed the message, Brother Cox," Ben Patton remarked.

"If the weather stays like this, you'll have all your crops planted in a few weeks," the pastor exclaimed in his usual deliberate voice.

"Weatherman is calling for more rain, and from the looks of things, I'd say we'll get it," Ben said, pointing toward the darkening sky. "Don't suppose I could get you to do a little plowing for me since you are through with your job for the week."

"All you people think I have to do is preach on Sundays and Wednesdays; that's just the beginning. It's you farmers that only work six months of the year."

"Least you could do is pray that the rain holds off a spell. You do have connections, don't you?" Ben asked.

"Close ones, don't you?"

Ben smiled at the familiar banter. A burley man of average height in his early sixties, Ben was not especially religious, but he had a deep respect for spiritual matters and people with religious convictions. He also had tremendous appreciation for the pastor who had designed the church building and carried out his plan with such dedication. He was organized and efficient; Ben admired that.

Ben was also impressed with the pastor's work ethic. Brother Cox had worked side by side with the other church members to complete the project. Ben watched him work, and his admiration grew into a deep respect.

Eve joined Ben and the pastor outside. "How about joining us for lunch?" she asked.

"Well, you know I could never turn down a home-cooked meal—especially yours," the pastor said with a laugh. "Just let me make sure Betty hasn't made other plans."

"I thought Jake was coming today," Ben said to Eve after the pastor walked away. It was more of a question.

"He said he would try, "Eve said defensively. "He probably got busy with something else."

"Phew!" Ben let out a sigh.

"Ben," Eve said, "just give him a little space."

Ben shook his head in disgust. "He needs to take responsibility and get on with his life."

"Hey, Eve!" the pastor's wife shouted. "Leroy told me we might get a home-cooked meal today."

"Betty, I am sure Leroy gets lots of cooking at home."

"He does," she replied, "but I think he likes your cooking better."

Chapter 7

Bobby Jack woke to the sound of thunder. He was startled at first, but laid back and listened as the rain beat a rhythmic tune on the roof of his trailer. He stretched. It was the first time he had been able to sleep in days. His head hurt from drinking too much at the party last night, but other than that, he felt good. He looked at the clock. It was almost noon. He had slept close to twelve hours. He couldn't remember the last time he had been able to sleep more than a few minutes at a time.

He got out of bed and slid into a pair of Jeans. He popped a couple aspirins into his mouth and washed them down with a glass of water. He was hungry. He tried to remember the last time he had eaten. He looked in the cabinet next to the sink to see if he had any food. There were several boxes of Cracker Jacks, and he ate two of them in rapid succession. A half-empty bottle of Coke, flat, was the only thing he had to drink besides water. He took a swallow, made a face, and finished the rest of the bottle. Today was going to be a busy day.

The rain had almost stopped by the time he was ready to leave. A fine mist continued to fall, like snow.

He crossed the creek and turned right on a poorly graded, one-lane gravel road that followed the creek to the foot of the mountain. The wind began to blow harder, turning leaves over and showing their silver sides. He passed the cemetery and the church and followed the winding road until he came to a trailer. It was the last dwelling in the Cove. The road ended, and the mountains towered high above.

Bobby Jack considered blowing the horn, but decided to get out and knock instead. The walkway was bordered with lilies and small dogwoods. The wind was beginning to gust, blowing the swing on the deck awkwardly.

Rusty Miller was still in bed when he heard the knock at the door. He rolled over and looked at the clock. It was 12:30 PM. He felt like he had just gone to sleep. "I'm coming!" he yelled after the third knock. He wasn't wearing a shirt. His stomach was lean and his arms muscular. "What the hell is going on?" he said, shielding his eyes from the bright sunlight.

"Rough night?" Bobby Jack asked, noting Rusty's short, uncombed hair, which stood straight up like a frightened cartoon character's.

"Yeah it was," Rusty said, buttoning his pants that until now had only been zipped.

"You got a few minutes to talk?" Bobby Jack asked.

"Yeah, come on in," Rusty said. "Preacher said you'd be coming by."

Bobby Jack went inside and sat on the couch. *What had Rusty said about Preacher saying he was coming by? When had Rusty talked to Preacher? Maybe it was at the party last night.* Bobby Jack wasn't sure, but he would figure it out later.

"So what's up?" Rusty asked.

Bobby Jack looked around the room. Everything was neat and in place. He thought about the squalor he lived in and felt guilty for not being as orderly.

"You working anywhere?" Bobby Jack asked.

"Not since I got laid off at the mines."

Bobby Jack looked surprised. Everyone said Rusty was fired, but if that was the way he wanted it to seem, it was cool with him.

"I got a way we can make a bunch of money," Bobby Jack said in a whisper.

"What you got on your mind?"

By the time Bobby Jack finished outlining the plan, he was certain he had a willing accomplice. "When you're poor, like me," Bobby Jack said, "nobody respects you. When I get enough money, I'll get my respect."

"Respect don't mean shit. Fear is the important thing," Rusty said. "When people fear you, you call the shots."

"I don't know about that," Bobby Jack said, "but I need to make this score."

"Who's going with you guys?"

"Reckon Martin would be interested?"

"Probably. I'll talk to him," Rusty said. "I'm supposed to see him later, anyway."

Bobby Jack stood to leave. A picture of Rusty and Shelby was sitting on the TV. She was beautiful—perfect, in fact. She had the most beautiful eyes he had ever seen. "She's too much of a woman for a Yankee like you," Bobby Jack said, pointing at the picture. "You ought to let me have a try."

They walked outside. "Country boy like you wouldn't know what to do with a real woman."

Bobby Jack climbed in his truck. "Be at Preacher's tomorrow night."

He backed out of the driveway. The sky was darker than before. Clouds raced across the sky, partially obscuring the sun and casting an eerie shadow on the mountain. A streak of lightening snaked across the western horizon. The rain had stopped for the time being, but the fresh smell of rain was in the air.

Chapter 8

A faint smile crossed Rusty's lips. Preacher's plan was coming together. He went back inside and fell on the bed. Damn, his head hurt. He looked at the clock again. No sense getting up. He picked up the picture of Shelby on the nightstand next to the clock. She was beautiful. He still remembered the first time he saw her. It was his first day at Booneville High School. His mother and father had divorced, and his mother had moved back home to the Cove. He wasn't happy about moving to the backwoods, but it didn't do him any good to complain. He had attended four different schools in the past three years. He wasn't anywhere long enough to make real friends, so moving wasn't that big of a deal.

Shelby had been in his third period American history class. Mr. Ladd had paired them together on a project, and they just seemed to click. Her boyfriend had broken up with her, and she was broken-hearted and lonely. He didn't have any friends, she needed someone to talk to, and soon they were together every moment.

Her parents hadn't liked him from the beginning. Maybe it was because he was a stranger. Her parents wanted her to go to college, but Rusty had talked her into getting married after graduation. Her parents were furious. His mother didn't care. She was glad to have him out of the house.

"What did Bobby Jack want?" Shelby asked as she walked into the room.

"Nothing, baby," he said, moving to the other side of the bed, taking her hand, and gently pulling her next to him. He stroked her hair tenderly. "I'm sorry about last night," he said. She shied away. "Sometimes I just get crazy."

"How could you do this?" she said, her voice cracking as she turned to face him.

"Oh, baby! I'm really sorry," he said, and reached out to kiss her. She jerked away.

"What's wrong? I said I was sorry, didn't I?"

"Yeah, Rusty. You're always sorry!"

"I won't ever hit you again. I promise."

"Yeah, I believe you. How many times have you told me that before?"

"This time it will be different. I promise."

"Rusty, you always promise that it will be different, but it never is."

"I can change—"

"You need help. You need to go to a counselor or something."

"I ain't crazy!"

"I didn't say you were. I just said that you need help."

"You think I'm crazy, don't you?"

"I know you're using crank—"

"What the hell difference does that make?"

"It sure doesn't help any."

"Why the hell do you care what I do?"

"You're my husband, and you have to get help or—"

The words hung in the air.

Rusty stood up. "Or what? You'll leave me? You remember what I told you would happen if you ever tried to leave me?"

"Rusty, please. I just want to talk to you about—"

"Damn bitch!" he shouted. He grabbed her and forced her to her back. "Sorry I ain't as good as Jake Patton." He spat the words. She struggled to free herself. He forced his lips against her sore mouth. Thunder rumbled in the distance.

Chapter 9

An hour later, Rusty drove down the creek road to the other side of the Cove. He stopped in front of a white frame house and blew the horn. The windows on the end of the house were covered with black plastic, and "No Trespassing" signs dotted the dwelling. A girl opened the screen door and waved. Rusty smiled and said, "Hey, Renee. Where's little brother?"

"Up at the barn," she said, walking toward the truck. Her shirt was tied in a knot, revealing a flat stomach, and her ample bosom pressed against the fabric.

"Looking good," Rusty said appraisingly, as he looked up and down her body, finally stopping at her breasts.

"See something you like?" she asked, leaning against his arm.

He felt her nipples against his skin. "Ain't got time for no fun and games right now," he said as his hands reached down and caressed her buttocks.

"I haven't seen you in three months, and you promised me we'd have some time together."

"I know," he said, "but soon it will be different."

"Promise?"

"Promise."

She gave him a quick kiss, and he backed out of the driveway and eased down a dirt path toward the barn.

Martin came out of the barn with a rooster under his arm. His head was completely shaved except for a shock of black hair that came out from the back of his head and hung in a ponytail. He wiped his eyes and squinted into the rays of sunlight that stabbed openings in the ominous clouds to see who was there. His pale, chalky complexion caused his green eyes to appear darker than they actually were. A pair of hoop earrings dangled in each ear.

"Is that what we are having for dinner?" Rusty asked.

"Hell, no! That's my best fighting rooster. He's beat just about every rooster in the Cove," Martin said in a rapid, staccato fashion, and then, as was his habit, repeated himself.

"So, what're you doing?" Rusty asked.

"Trying to get my roosters ready for the fight," Martin answered. "Gotta get them ready for a fight."

"What kind of chicken do you call that?" Rusty asked, noticing its small head and yellow legs.

"That'd be an Allen Roundhead," Martin said proudly. "Best fighting rooster there is, Allen Roundhead."

He sat the rooster on the ground. It flapped its wings a couple times, as if it were stretching, and strutted off. "Got a lot of spring in its legs and some damned wicked spurs. Course we put shanks on. Got big spurs, but you need shanks."

Rusty explained Preacher's plan, but Martin didn't appear interested. "I got plenty of money right here," he explained, pulling a roll of bills from his dirty, black jeans and showing them to Rusty.

"You could have plenty more in a few days," Rusty said.

"Plenty more trouble, too. Plenty trouble."

"We got it lined up. Shouldn't be no trouble."

"My daddy always told me you could get in more trouble in a minute than you could get out of in a lifetime. He ought to know. He's been sent up three times."

"Just come listen to Preacher," Rusty said.

"You want to go to the fight?" Martin asked.

Rusty had heard about the cockfights but had never been. "What time?"

"Fighting starts at four."

"Where at?"

"Damn," Martin said. "How long you been living here?"

"Too damn long."

"Well, you ought to know where the cockfights are by now," Martin said. "They are up past the sawmill at the Dent place."

Rusty tried to recall what it was that people said about the Dent family. He'd heard Preacher talk about them before, but he couldn't recall the story.

"What's that that Preacher told me about the Dent place?"

"Preacher is always talking some garbage," Martin said.

"Did one of them get killed or something?"

"Yeah, a long time ago. Old man Buck Dent. This was a damn long time ago—back in the Depression or something. He was a big talker. Didn't know when to keep his mouth shut. He knew where some people had a moonshine still and was telling everybody about it. One morning, when he was starting to market with a couple hens and some vegetables, somebody bushwhacked him in the road in front of his house. Shot him from two directions with 12 ga. shotguns. Nearly blew him in half. People said there were chicken feathers splattered with blood all over the road."

"I remember Preacher talking about it."

"People say Bobby Jack's grandpa had something to do with it. He went crazy after it happened. I've heard my grandmother say he used to go around and drink water out of mud holes."

"That is crazy."

"So you gonna go to the fight?"

"Yeah, I ain't got nothing better to do."

"I got to go check on my garden," Martin said. "Come on and walk to the cave with me. I got to check my garden."

Near the entrance to the cave, Rusty saw several rows of plastic pots. Growing in each pot were plants that Rusty recognized immediately. Each plant was about a foot tall and tied to a small stick with pieces of yarn to keep them straight.

"Damn, you got a stash here." Rusty said. "Where did you get all these plants?"

Martin opened a sack half full of tiny, black seeds. "I got plenty more where these came from. I'm gonna plant a whole field full. I'll be high from now on. I got plenty more."

That would probably be true. Martin lived to get high. He had smoked pot for the first time when he was twelve years old. His old man, Zack, had a small patch growing down by the creek. Martin talked a couple boys into trying it with him. When his old man found out, he whipped Martin with a horsewhip for messing with his patch. When Zack went to jail, Martin began growing his own. Over the years, he had tried about everything.

They walked down to the creek, where Martin had dug about thirty big holes. He ran a plastic pipe from the creek to the bottom of the hole so the roots could get water.

"What do you think of my irrigation system?" Martin asked. "What do you think?"

Rusty was amazed at how elaborate the system was. "Damn, boy! Are you some kind of engineer?"

"I do a lot of reading," Martin said. "You can learn a lot in books."

"Where the hell do you read about stuff like this?"

"Got this idea from *Popular Mechanics*."

"Growing pot?"

"Well, not about the pot, but about how to set up the irrigation."

"What are you reading now?"

"*The Grapes of Wrath*."

"You going into wine-making next?"

Martin shook his head in disbelief. "You have heard of *The Grapes of Wrath*?"

"What happened to these?" Rusty asked, ignoring Martin's question and pointing to several dead plants lying on the ground.

"Those are male plants. You have to remove them before they pollinate if you want a good smoke. Otherwise, you get some of that weak shit like you sell."

Rusty shrugged. Apparently, there was a lot he could learn from Martin. "Are you trying to corner the pot market?" he asked. "Maybe you'll be the Al Capone of pot."

Martin laughed, but Rusty wasn't too far off. Martin had always idolized his uncle, Ralph Hogan, a small-time criminal who had caught Martin's attention by driving a fancy red sports car. Ralph had gone to prison when he was about Martin's age. The first time, he did a year for stealing two cows and selling them to a fellow in Woodbury. The second time he was convicted, he did seven years for counterfeiting.

Once out of prison, Ralph always seemed to have money. He told everyone who would listen about his stay in Brushy Mountain State Prison. He claimed to have helped James Earl Ray escape the first time he tried. He also said Ray alleged that he had been paid a half a million dollars to kill Martin Luther King. The people who paid for the hit were supposed to have someone drive Ray to Mobile after he escaped. From there, he would travel to Columbia by private boat.

After he escaped, they failed to show up at the appointed place. Ray was forced to try an escape through the mountains, an almost impossible task. He was captured shortly thereafter.

Once in custody, Ray threatened to write a book exposing those involved in the conspiracy. Soon, Ray's brother received a large amount of cash. Ray wrote a book, *The Tennessee Waltz*, but it made no mention of the people who paid him.

Ralph claimed to be James Earl Ray's right-hand man. According to him, they got anything they wanted in prison. Martin wanted that power.

"Be at Preacher's Monday at 8:00," Rusty said.

"I'll be there," Martin said, picking up his rooster and putting him back under his arm.

Rusty walked back to his truck. Everything was coming together. He took one look back at Martin. He had placed the rooster on the ground and walked around it. Every once in a while, he would jump toward the rooster, and it would dodge deftly out of the way.

"Crazy," Rusty said to himself. He backed out of the driveway and headed toward home. The sky was black and threatening.

Chapter 10

"Ben, I tell you, I just love this place," the Pastor said, admiring the view from the front yard.

"Yeah, it's not bad," Ben replied, trying to hide his pride.

"Honey, would you have still married me if we had to live in a little shack like this?" the pastor asked his wife teasingly.

"I don't know," she replied. "Those two-bedroom parsonages are pretty hard to beat." The two hugged.

It was a huge, two-story, white frame house with a tin roof. Large white columns supported a porch that stretched all the way around the house. Swings and wicker rockers made it the perfect place to sit and read a book or visit with friends.

"Come on in," Ben said, opening the door. "Make yourself at home; I'll help Eve for a minute. The Braves are playing if you want to watch the game."

"I've kind of given up on baseball since the strike," the pastor replied.

"Anything I can do to help you, Eve?" Betty asked.

"No, I just have to put the roast in the oven to warm. Everything is done."

The pastor sat down on the couch. His wife walked around the room, admiring the furniture. She walked over to the huge fireplace and stared at the size and grandeur of the rockwork. "I just love mountain stone," she said.

"Betty, you know it is a sin to covet," he said with a laugh.

"Leroy, I'm not coveting, but it is nice." They both laughed. The pastor joined his wife as they looked around. The hall was lined with pictures.

Ben reentered the room and noticed them looking at a picture of a horse. "That's Midas Touch."

"Very pretty horse," the pastor said.

"Do you know much about walking horses?'

"Not really anything," the pastor replied. "We have learned since we have been here that this is walking horse country."

"The walking horse got its start just up the road from here. Most of the walking horses today are descendants of the Wilson Allen stallion that belonged to Frank Wilson, who lived just past the church."

"Midas Touch must have been a good horse from the looks of all those ribbons," Betty said, looking closer at the picture.

"That picture was taken at the National Walking Horse Show in Shelbyville. Midas Touch was named Grand Champion."

"Who are the people in the picture?" Betty asked.

"This fellow here," Ben said, pointing to a small, wiry fellow, "is Jimmy Gray, our trainer. This is Wince Biggio, who rode for us in all the shows, and that thin young man there is me."

"You haven't changed," Betty said.

"I am thirty years older and thirty pounds heavier," Ben said with a laugh.

"Which one is Jake?" Betty asked, looking at a collage of football pictures.

"Number eleven," Ben replied. "All those were taken when he was playing for Vanderbilt." They looked at the pictures. The first three showed Jake throwing passes; the next three showed Jake scoring touchdowns, and the final one showed Jake with both hands in the air signaling a touchdown. The University of Tennessee checkerboard end zone was clearly visible in the background.

"Didn't Eve tell me Jake got hurt playing football?" Betty asked.

"Yeah, he messed up his knee at Ole Miss. He never was able to play after that."

"That was really unfortunate," the pastor interjected. "From what everyone around here says, we might be watching him on TV today if he hadn't been injured."

Ben smiled. "Maybe," he said, "but it is a big jump from college to the NFL."

"What's this?" Betty asked, looking at a framed magazine article.

"*Sports Illustrated* did an article on the Vanderbilt football team. They started the season 7-0 for the first time in school history and made the AP top ten. Jake just happened to be the quarterback."

"Who is this?" Betty asked, looking at a smaller picture.

"The little fellow here is Danny Spencer. He was fourteen and dying from leukemia. Dr. Stein, who was the head of the oncology department at Vanderbilt, told Jake about the young man's condition. Jake went to visit him, and they became fast friends. When Danny was able, he went everywhere with Jake."

"That was so thoughtful," Betty said.

"The odd thing about this picture is that Jake is giving Danny a jersey, but it isn't a Vanderbilt jersey. Danny was a big Tennessee fan. He loved Peyton Manning, the former Volunteer quarterback. Jake knew that Rob Sloan, a former Vanderbilt basketball coach who is now the athletic director, was good friends with Peyton's dad, Archie. Jake had Rob contact Archie, and Archie explained the situation to Peyton.

"When the Colts were in town playing the Titans, Peyton called Jake and told him he had something for Danny. Peyton went with Jake to see Danny. He was in the hospital after having a tough time with chemotherapy. Peyton took one of his old Tennessee jerseys and gave it to Danny.

"Danny was so excited. He wore it over his hospital gown. We thought he might never take it off."

"What happened to Danny?" the pastor asked.

"He died a couple years ago. The cancer was just too far advanced. You know what? He was buried in a football jersey."

"The jersey that Peyton gave him?" the pastor asked.

Ben shook his head. "Jake's gold Vanderbilt jersey. It was Danny's last request," Ben said his voice cracking.

"This is our oldest son Chase and our daughter Amy," Eve said pointing to large oil paintings . She continued to explain who was in each picture and what their connection was to the family. There was one of Ben and her before they were married. Ben was sitting on a split rail fence, and she was standing behind him, posing bashfully. They were both young and good-looking.

"That was many moons ago," Eve said, laughing at herself. "Ben is a couple years older than me, and he had gone north to find work. We wrote each other all the time, but I hardly ever got to see him. This was one of those times he was home for a few days."

"I had to go somewhere to find work during those days. There wasn't anything to do around here," Ben said, as if defending himself.

"Who is this with Jake at the prom?" Betty asked.

"Shelby Parker," Eve replied. "They dated for a long time."

"Pretty girl," the pastor said. "They made a cute couple."

"Jake wanted to marry her," Eve said.

"We wanted Jake to go to school, play ball, and get an education. They were just kids," Ben said.

"We were just kids, too," Eve said. Ben remained silent, deep in thought.

"Dinner should be ready, if anyone is hungry," Eve said, breaking the silence.

"I'm starved," the pastor replied, sniffing the air to smell the baking bread. "I can't wait to taste that roast. Sunday dinner at the Pattons' is always a treat."

The table was a smorgasbord of vegetables cooked in various ways—green beans, fried okra, squash casserole, and carrots and potatoes cooked with the roast. After giving thanks for the bounty, everyone began passing bowls of food, not adhering to any particular direction. They ate in relative silence, except for comments on how good everything tasted.

"Save room for some blackberry cobbler," Eve said, as everyone appeared to finish.

Before anyone could answer, the sound of a vehicle caught their attention. "Probably Jake," Eve said.

"Did you save any for me?" Jake Patton asked as he strode into the dining room.

"We left a little," Ben said, looking at the abundance of food still on the table.

Jake walked over and kissed his mom's cheek before turning his attention to the others in the room.

"You know Brother Cox and his wife Betty don't you?" Eve asked.

"Sure," Jake said. "Great to see you folks."

"You're late," Ben said. Ben Patton was never late for anything, and tardiness was hard for him to accept in other people, especially his son.

Eve brought Jake a plate, and he began to tell them what had happened the day before.

"Is the boy going to be all right?" Betty asked.

"After they got him out of the gulf, I took Allison to the hospital. She was pretty shaken up. They checked her out, and she seemed okay. The boy is going to be in the hospital a while. He fell some forty feet and landed in a pile of rocks."

"Oh, my!" the pastor exclaimed. "That can't be good."

"His leg is broken in at least two places; one is a compound fracture. He also has broken ribs and a fractured wrist. He had lost a lot of blood. The doctor said he wouldn't have made it much longer."

"We'll certainly put him on our prayer list at church," the pastor said.

"It's a good thing she found you when she did," Eve said, shaking her head. "I've told you how dangerous it is to climb, especially by yourself."

"It will take a long time, but they seem to think he will make a complete recovery," Jake said.

"Does he have family around here?" Betty asked.

"He has an uncle in Sewanee. I went back to the hospital to check on him. That's why I am late."

"I've heard that you played quarterback at Vanderbilt," the preacher said.

"Just a short time, but it was a lot of fun."

"I played football in high school." the pastor said. "It was always my dream to play college football, but there wasn't much demand for 160-pound linebackers, even back in my day."

"I hate linebackers," Jake said with a laugh. "One of them ended my career. I guess that makes you one of the bad guys."

"I always hit quarterbacks high and drove them into the ground," the pastor replied. "I'd never hit a puny QB low."

Jake laughed aloud. "Dad said you were a cut up."

"What makes you think I'm kidding?" the pastor said with a straight face before bursting into a big grin.

"All right, you two are going to have to calm down so we can eat dessert," Eve said, beaming that Jake and Brother Cox were getting along so well.

"No dessert for me," Betty said. "I'm stuffed."

"Sounds like more for us, Leroy," Ben said. The pastor laughed in agreement.

The men ate blackberry cobbler and talked sports while Betty and Eve swapped recipes. After everyone finished, Jake helped the ladies take the dishes to the sink. Ben and the pastor went back to the living room.

When Jake went to join them, the pastor was looking at an old musket above the mantle.

"That gun belonged to my great-grandfather, Jim Patton," Ben said. "He was killed by a bunch of bushwhackers back during the War Between the States."

"We had a lot of the same thing out in Kansas," the pastor said. "Between Quantrill's Raiders and Lane's Redlegs, no one was safe."

"They strung him up right here on this hill," Ben said. "His family had to watch while they tortured him. He died trying to protect his family and this place from killers and thieves. Sometimes I sit on the porch and try to imagine what it must have been like during those times."

"It's hard for us to picture what things were like in those days," the pastor said.

"I don't believe in ghosts," Ben said, "but somehow I feel his presence all around this place."

"It's a shame that they got away with robbing and killing people," the pastor said.

"Well I'm not sure they got away totally free. Brady, the man that led the raiders, died a terrible death. After the war, many Confederate veterans returned home and were mighty upset at what had happened to their loved ones while they were gone. It wasn't long before masked riders began to exact revenge."

"The KKK?" The pastor asked.

"Not sure they called themselves that, but some of the men, like my grandfather, had ridden with General Forrest. Anyway, Brady, the leader of the bunch that lynched my great-grandfather, was trying to get out of the country before the vigilantes found him. He was at a railroad depot in Decherd. No one knows for sure what happened, but they found his body riddled with bullets."

"As bad as it sounds, he probably got what he deserved," Betty said as she walked into the room. The pastor looked at her disapprovingly and shook his head.

"Some people thought that my grandfather had something to do with it, but I don't think anyone knew for sure. He never said anything to me about it."

"How long have the Pattons owned this place?"

"Moses Patton came here in 1805. He had twenty-five thousand acres of land he had acquired through land grants. He was given some land for his service during the American Revolution, and he bought as much as he could afford."

Eve joined them in the living room. She carried a silver tray with a pot of coffee and poured each of them a cup.

"Ahhh, wonderful," the pastor said.

"Cream or sugar, anyone?" Eve asked. They declined, except for Jake, who poured a generous amount of each.

"Ben, I don't know what to think about anybody who takes cream in their coffee, do you?" the pastor said with a wink.

Ben shook his head. Jake hung his head in mock shame.

"That's an amazing amount of land," the pastor said. "Did you hear that, Betty? The Pattons have lived here almost two hundred years."

"I don't think we have ever lived anywhere ten years," she replied.

"Well, not exactly two hundred years on the same spot," Ben said. "Moses built a cabin closer to the river. The house my great-grandfather Jim built was located here, though it faced a different direction. It was burned during the war. Times were hard during the reconstruction. My grandpa, Joshua, was forced to sell the land bit by bit to take care of his mother and two sisters, who both lost husbands during the fighting."

"How did you manage to get it back in the family?"

"I know Lucifer's great sin was pride," Ben said, "so I want you to know I am not boasting."

Jake and Eve looked at each other and smiled. They had heard the story many times before, and the opening was always the same.

"Don't get Dad started," Jake said. "You will get another history lecture on the saga of the Patton family."

"I'd love to hear it," the pastor said. "Go ahead, Ben. Don't hold back."

"Maybe some other time," Ben said. "I'm too full to give you all a history lesson now."

"At least give them the *Reader's Digest* version," Jake said.

Ben cleared his throat. "My grandfather would sit me on his knee and tell me about the history of the Pattons in America. He felt bad about having to sell the farm off to survive. He made me promise I would buy as much of it back as possible if I ever got the chance. He had kept ten acres, and my father was able to buy forty more, but the bulk of it remained untouchable."

"Anyone want their coffee warmed?" Eve asked. The pastor held out his cup for a refill.

"I bought it back a piece at a time. Of course, I paid too much for it, but it was my burning ambition to get as much back as I could."

"Dad only wants the land that joins him," Jake said with a laugh.

Ben looked a little sheepish. "I knew I could never own all of it, but I wanted to get as much as I could around the old home place."

"How much land do you have now?" Betty asked.

"About twenty-five hundred acres at the Patton place. I got a couple other small pieces of property that aren't connected."

"Boy, that's a lot of land," the pastor said.

"About a tenth of what was the original homestead."

"Still a lot of land," the pastor said, shaking his head.

"Sorry if I bored you," Ben said. "I get carried away when I start talking about it. This land was so important to my family. My ancestors bled and died to settle it and defend it and getting it back in the family has been a goal for much of my life."

"You didn't bore us at all," the pastor said. "Looks like you achieved your goal and more."

"He certainly did," Eve said.

"I hope there will be Pattons on this farm for a long time to come," Ben said, looking intently at Jake.

Jake turned away and looked away at the mountains in the distance. The wind beat the limbs of the maple trees in the front yard back and forth like whips. Drops of rain began to fall on the roof.

Chapter 11

The clouds in the sky were growing more menacing. Streaks of lightning gave all indications that a thunderstorm was about to hit. Trees bent in the wind.

Bobby Jack drove back down the twisting road. *Damn nasty weather.* He passed the Winton Place, where rooster pens and junk cars served as the only landscaping.

He drove unhurriedly, thinking about his life. He had been married once. That ended two years ago. He had a kid, Dylan, who was three. He hadn't seen him in almost a year. Dylan's mother, Angela, had taken him and moved away from the Cove. She didn't even want any child support; she just wanted to get away.

Dylan had a wild head of hair like Bobby Jack. He had named him for Bob Dylan. *Like a Rolling Stone.* That's what he was. He missed Dylan, but he knew he was better off. Angela had married some dude, and he had a job and was good to Dylan.

Bobby Jack headed back toward Preacher's house. There was no sense in going home; it was lonely with no one there.

Preacher had to have more than he was giving out earlier. Just a little was all he needed. Preacher was saving the good stuff and trying to pawn weed to him.

Bobby Jack turned down the road toward Preacher's house. A burnt orange Sentra pulled out of Preacher's driveway and met him. Bobby Jack moved over to let the vehicle by. A couple of teenagers, a girl and boy, waved uneasily. Bobby Jack had seen them before but couldn't remember where. Damn, his memory was getting bad.

He parked in the yard and walked toward the door. He stepped on the sagging porch. It creaked from his weight.

"Where you at, Preacher?" he yelled, and opened the screen door.

"Back here getting some more wood. I'll be out in a minute."

Bobby Jack sat down on the front porch, leaning back against the wall. After a few minutes, Preacher shuffled out.

"Looks like you had company," Bobby Jack said in a questioning manner.

"Couple kids from Booneville," Preacher replied.

"I need some shit," Bobby Jack said, almost pleading.

"Martin is making some good stuff."

"I need it now."

"I got some grass," Preacher said. "You want some grass?"

"Naw, I need more than weed."

Preacher stood up and stretched. "I got a little shit, but it ain't no count," he said.

"Just a little will do me 'til tonight."

"Let's go inside."

Preacher went to a drawer in the kitchen, got out a glass pipe, and handed it to Bobby Jack. "Ain't much left but a little fog in the pipe."

Bobby Jack looked at it, disappointed. "Ain't enough to get roaring," he said.

"I got this," Preacher said, holding up a small bag. "Martin said this ain't worth fooling with."

"Where'd you get it?"

"Can't tell you everything, partner. I just sell it to locals that don't care what they get."

"It ain't Martin's."

"Hell, no!" Preacher said. "He got mad at me for having it—said it was going to ruin his reputation as a chef."

The crunch of gravel on the road caught Preacher's attention. "Hold on," Preacher said, putting the bag back in the drawer. "Looks like we got company."

The car stopped behind Bobby Jack's truck. Two teenage girls got out.

Preacher opened the screen door and walked outside. Booby Jack stood in the doorway behind him.

"Hello, ladies," Preacher said as they approached the porch. "You better get on up here out of the rain."

"Hey, Preacher!" one of them said, brushing her raven black hair out of her eyes, "What's going on?"

"Not much," Preacher said. "My friend and I were enjoying the day until the damn rain started. Who's that you got with you, Misty?"

"This is Donna," Misty said. "We have been buds a long time."

Donna smiled revealing a stud tongue ring. "What kind of decoration do you call that?" Preacher asked.

The girls giggled.

"Preacher, you gotta keep up with the times," Misty said.

"Don't it hurt?" Bobby Jack asked.

"A little when they did it," Donna said.

"And there's all kind of things it good for," Misty said, smiling innocently.

"Now that I'd like to hear about," Preacher said.

Misty laughed. "Look at my new belly ring," she said, raising her shirt to reveal a diamond on the navel of her flat stomach.

"Looks good," Preacher said. "Got anymore under there to show me?"

"Nope!" Misty said, lifting her shirt high enough to expose her bare breasts.

"Damn, she's right, Preacher," Bobby Jack said, flashing a toothy grin. "She ain't got nothing else on under there."

"What kind a tattoo was that?" Bobby Jack asked, hoping to get another look at her skin. She raised her shirt again, revealing a butterfly just bellow her belly button disappearing into her tight fitting jeans,

"Nice," Preacher said.

"You are my inspiration, Preacher," she said, pointing to the tattoos on his arms.

"Always glad to help," Preacher said.

The two girls giggled. "Do you have anything?" Misty asked.

"Depends on what you got for me," Preacher said.

The girls giggled again. "So what ya got?" Misty said.

"You got money?" Preacher asked.

"Not much, but we might work out a deal with you, like before."

"Both of you?" Preacher asked, interested.

"If that's what you want," Misty said.

"What about your friend there?" Preacher said. "She hasn't had much to say."

"She's game," Misty said.

Preacher turned to look at her, giving her an appraising gaze. "How old are you, anyway?"

"Old enough," Donna said.

"And just how old is that?"

"Eighteen."

"You sure you're eighteen?"

"I'm sure."

"Come on in, ladies," Preacher said. "We'll see what we can work out."

Bobby Jack opened the door and ushered them in. Once inside, he closed the door and locked it. Misty went to the bed and sat down. Preacher took the bag he had shown Bobby Jack out of the drawer. He reached in his pocket and retrieved the pipe.

"This is all I got," he said, showing them the bag. "It's yours if you want it."

Both girls eyed the bag, excited. Misty got off the bed and walked to where Preacher was standing. Donna followed her lead.

"You're the best," Misty said, removing her shirt.

Preacher handed her the bag. She smiled. Preacher took hold of her arm and pulled her close to him. He grabbed her hair roughly and kissed her deeply. His hand fondled her body. They fell onto the bed.

"What are you waiting for?" Preacher asked Bobby Jack, who was still standing by the door.

Donna turned toward Bobby Jack and began removing her clothes. Thunder crashed, rattling the windows.

Chapter 12

Dennis struggled to remove the final brake pad on his truck. The brakes had been making a noise for a while, but he hadn't found the time to check it. The nuts had rusted.

He grunted and cursed as he tugged to loosen its hold.

He cursed himself for letting Bobby Jack talk him into such a fool plan. Robbing Ben Patton was crazy. The Pattons probably had all types of security. Dennis didn't really know Ben Patton. He had spoken to him a few times when they ran into each other. His pa always talked about Ben.

He heard the sound of a vehicle. If it was Bobby Jack, he was going to tell him to forget his dumb ass plan and think of something else. At least, he could tell him he wanted no part of it.

The truck pulled into his driveway, but it wasn't Bobby Jack. Dennis wiped the grease off his hands. "How are you doing, Mr. Tucker?" Dennis said, recognizing the man in the truck.

"Fair, just fair," was the mumbled reply.

"What can I help you with?"

"My truck is making a funny noise, and I thought you might know what's wrong with it."

Dennis walked to the passenger's side and got in. "Drive it down the road and let's see."

"Hear that?"

"Yeah," Dennis said after they had driven only a short distance. "You need a clutch."

"How much that going to cost?"

"Probably about three hundred bucks."

"Is that including putting it in?"

Dennis looked at Mr. Tucker and shook his head. He knew the old man didn't have much money, but he wasn't going to do it free. The old man was crazy and didn't need to be driving anyway. "Tell you what, Mr. Tucker—you get the clutch, and I will put it on for you. You can pay me what you think it is worth."

"Fair enough," he said when Dennis got out. "I'll be back."

Dennis didn't know if he would come back or not. He really didn't care. If the old man brought the clutch back, he'd fix it for him, but he was sure he'd never get any money for it.

He hadn't checked on his mother in a while and thought he'd better look in on her. "Can I get you something, Mama?" Dennis asked, closing the door behind him. His mother was sitting in her recliner, rocking back and forth. She continued to stare out the window, her watery, green eyes frozen in the past.

Dennis walked over and stood in front of her. It was something he had started doing in hopes of bringing her out of her trance. "Why are you wearing that?" Dennis asked, pointing at the red-striped blouse she was wearing.

"Henry got it for me last Christmas," she said at last, acknowledging he was in the room. She held out a nametag. It was old and faded, but he could still see RUBY, all in capital letters, on it—her nametag when she worked at Kroger's.

Dennis shook his head. The blouse was old and threadbare. She wore a plaid wool skirt that clashed violently with her top. His mother never had a lot of money, but she was particular about the way she dressed. She would have been embarrassed for anyone to see her if she were in her right mind. Of course, she wasn't, and never would be again.

He needed help with her, but his sister was either too busy or lazy to help. She hardly ever came to visit, much less help. She had three kids of her own and that took time, but this was her mother, too. He shouldn't have to do everything himself.

"I cooked dinner for you and Henry. You better get it before it gets cold," she said.

Dennis went to the stove. The stove eyes were on, but the pots sitting on them were empty.

"Damn," he said, after touching the handle of one of the pans. He ran cold water over his hand until the burning stopped. "Mama, you can't put pans on the stove without anything in them."

"I cooked you and Henry some taters and beans."

"Mama, look at the stove." He helped her from the chair and led her to the stove. "See, they're empty."

She looked at the stove with a blank expression and walked back to her chair. She picked up a worn magazine and sat back down.

"You're going to start a fire. I've told you not to turn on the stove when I'm not in here."

"Henry was hungry, and you know how he hates to wait."

"Ma, you're going to set the house on fire. I mean it. Don't touch the stove if I'm not here."

"I've been cooking on that stove for twenty-five years."

"But you're not well—"

"Not well! That's a bunch of hogwash. I feel fine."

"Ma, I don't want you to set the house on fire. I'll cook when we need something."

"I've cooked all my life. Ask your Pa. He'll tell you I know how to cook."

"I know you can cook, but sometimes you forget things."

"I don't need no teenager telling me what to do!"

"Ma, I ain't a teenager any more. I'm twenty-eight years old."

She turned back and stared out the window. Dennis washed his hands, peeled some potatoes, and put them on the stove to boil. His mother was still a young woman, but she had given up when his father died. He didn't know the medical reasoning behind it, but he was sure she wouldn't be like this if his father were alive.

His father had worked in the coalmines as long as Dennis could remember. Most of that time, he operated an old, worn out drill. At times, it shook so violently that it threw him against the walls. The dust suppressors were constantly breaking down, and the dust was suffocating. Henry told him that sometimes it got so bad he had to go out in the fresh air to puke. When he was able to catch his breath, the boss would come by and send him back in again.

He came home at night looking like he had been sprayed with oil and rolled in black flour. The last few years he worked, he was unable to walk up the steps to get into the house without stopping to rest.

Henry's brother George was killed when a slab of coal collapsed. Henry's left hand had been mangled in the same accident. He was never able to open it, and it remained clinched in a permanent fist. Because of the injury and his declining health, Henry was given a less strenuous job. The change cut his hours from an average of sixty a week to forty.

Afraid he would not be able to provide for his family, he returned to operating the press. His hand was practically useless, so he had to pry his fingers open and place it around the handle of the drill in order to operate it.

On Christmas Eve, he had his first bad attack. He came home from work with a pain in his chest. Ruby persuaded him, with great difficulty, to go to the emergency room. The doctors ruled out a heart attack, but x-rays revealed that his lungs were severely damaged.

The doctor tried to convince him to quit mining. "Only way I know to provide for my family," he said, and returned to the mines. For a while, he wore a paper mask, but it was little help. He was barely able to walk, but could sit and run the drill in the endless clouds of coal dust.

Six months later, his lungs totally collapsed. He was forced to carry an oxygen tank with him everywhere he went. He never completely recovered. He had a few good days, but more bad ones. He said he knew the risks when he started working in the mines, so he had no one to blame but himself. Ruby disagreed. She blamed the coal companies for not protecting their employees. Regardless, it mattered little for Henry or his family. He died a year later.

Out of the Darkness

"What did you do with my watch?"

"Ma, I haven't seen your watch," Dennis said.

"I saw you come in here and get it off the dresser just a minute ago," she said, twisting the brooch on her blouse back and forth in rapid jerks.

"Ma, why would I want to take your watch?"

"'Cause yours tore up, and you want to wear mine."

"I don't even wear a watch, and I sure wouldn't wear yours."

She mumbled something Dennis couldn't understand, marched to her room, and closed the door.

Dennis ignored her and went about cooking. He set the table, making sure to place the silverware on a napkin, and not a paper towel. His mother hated when he used paper towels. He poured iced tea in the good glasses and made sure the salt and pepper were on the table.

He went to her bedroom door and knocked. "Ma, supper is ready."

There wasn't a reply. "Ma, you better eat before supper gets cold."

"I ain't hungry," she sullenly replied through the closed door.

"Okay, I am going to eat by myself."

The door creaked open. His mother looked out from behind the door. "We don't have company, do we?" she asked.

"No, it's just us."

She came out and walked briskly to the table. She stared at the place settings and smiled. "Everything looks good, don't it?" she said.

"It sure does, Ma."

"Well, you better get to eating. I hate to cook and nobody eat. Where's Henry?"

"Ma, you know Daddy's—"

Before he could finish, she walked into the back room, calling Henry's name.

Dennis didn't try to stop her. He had been through this before. She got angry with him if he stopped her before she finished searching for Henry.

Michael Clinton Oliver

She came back inside, still calling his name. The heel of her shoe caught on the throw rug in the living room. She tumbled awkwardly, grabbing the air for something to catch her fall. She landed on a small, wooden bookrack. Her hip and shoulder took the brunt of the fall.

Chapter 13

Martin placed the rooster in a pen with a covered top, went into the barn, and got some feed. He rolled oats and a small pat of hamburger meat into balls and stacked them in a yellow plastic bucket. Once he had used up all the meat, he placed the remaining oats back in a barrel and walked to the field, where dozens of rooster pens were lined like miniature apartment buildings.

The roosters were tethered to a stake in the pen, their tethers long enough to allow them access to the entire pen. Martin gave each rooster a ball of the oat-rolled meat.

"Hello, Flash," he said as a rooster pranced out of his house. "You better win me some money today." The rooster strutted around the pen; its bright feathers radiant and glossy in the sun's rays. Martin took a bottle out of his pocket and shook it. He used the eyedropper to pull some of the greenish liquid out of the bottle and began giving it to each of the roosters he had planned to take to the fight. "Drink up," he said, looking once again at the bottle. The label was solid black with the words "Pure Aggression" written in dark red, like dripping blood.

Martin loaded his roosters into the back of his truck. He drove to the Corner Café. Several cars and trucks were sitting outside, along with three muddy red four-wheelers. He got out and strolled inside. People were shooting pool in the back room. He walked over to where a buxom brunette was wiping a table. "Lindsey, you 'bout ready to go?" he asked.

"Give me a few minutes. We had a bunch of people come in late, and I got to clean up."

"Hurry up; I don't want to be late." He walked back to the pool tables. A couple guys he knew were standing around watching.

"What's happening, man?" a man asked when he walked up. The man had premature gray hair and looked like an aging hippie.

"Not much, Tommy," Martin replied. "Who's the new dude?" he asked, pointing at one of the guys shooting pool.

"Dude's name is James Berry, he's Larry Payne's cousin. He's from Nashville. Everybody calls him Snake. Man, he can shoot."

"He'll have a tough time beating Greg," Martin said, noting the big, stocky player eyeing the table.

"I got twenty dollars says he beats Greg this game."

"You're on," Martin said.

They watched intently as the game ebbed and flowed. Greg seemed to have the game in hand, but scratched and gave the new guy a chance. Snake was rail thin, with dark hair and long sideburns; he seemed to slide from shot to shot, not picking up his feet and wasting little time to aim. He sank the six ball in the corner pocket and left himself with a straight-in shot at the eight ball. He promptly sank it, and the game was over.

Martin paid while someone racked the balls, and they began again. "Want another twenty?" Tommy asked.

"Make it fifty?"

"It's your money."

Snake broke, but didn't make anything. Greg had several shots to choose from. With slow, deliberate movements, he knocked the thirteen ball in the side pocket and the nine ball into the corner. Left with a difficult shot, he managed to bank the twelve ball in the corner, but hooked himself behind the four ball. After Greg missed the next shot, Snake went to work on the solids. He made the one ball, four ball, and six ball in succession. Every shot he made appeared easy. Martin began to realize that even though Greg might be able to make the difficult shot, the new guy shot better and left himself with better chances. He finally missed with just one ball left on the table.

Greg made three straight shots, but shot too hard on the fourth, and the fifteen ball rattled out of the corner pocket.

Everyone was quiet. Snake slid the five ball into the corner pocket, and the cue ball came to rest with the eight ball lined in the other corner. Martin paid the fifty dollars before Snake sank the final shot. Lindsey was just finishing up when he went back to the dining area.

She talked the entire time it took to drive to the Dent place. Martin half-listened. He had lost seventy dollars on those stupid pool games. The entry fee was twenty dollars a rooster. That meant he only had four hundred and twenty dollars to bet on the rooster fights.

He lit a joint and handed it to her. She inhaled deeply. "I need to give Mama some money for the kids, and Ray don't pay me for work until Friday."

Lindsey was just twenty, but she had two kids that her folks raised. Martin wasn't sure who their daddy was, but he knew it wasn't him. She always wanted money from him because they needed something. He gave her money when he had it, but he doubted the kids ever saw it. When she had money, she blew it up her nose. "When Flash wins," Martin said, "we'll have plenty of money."

Lindsey smiled, leaned over, and began kissing his neck. He pulled her closer to him, feeling the heat of her body. Her hand caressed his thigh as he fumbled to undo her blouse. "As soon as this is over, I am going to take good care of you," she said in a seductive tone, her voice emphasizing "good."

They drove to the end of the road, crossed Dry Creek, and continued on an old logging road. The road was rough, but they made it with little difficulty. At the top of the hill was the old home place. The only evidence that a house once occupied the spot was a chimney that still stood after years of neglect.

Several other vehicles were already parked in the field. Martin removed his portable cages and carried his roosters.

"Here comes the man to beat," a man in overalls said when he saw Martin approach.

Martin held up the cage Flash was in. "You fellas better not bet against this here rooster. Flash done whupped every rooster's ass in this cove," he said and repeated himself as he did when he got excited. "Flash done whupped every one."

"Couple new roosters here today," the man said, rubbing his scraggly gray chin whiskers. "Might get interesting."

Martin paid his entry fee to a man in a denim shirt and red baseball cap and took his roosters to the pit area. The pit was a 10' by 10' section dug out of the earth. Rough-hewn planks lined the sides to prevent it from caving in. While Martin got everything set up, Rusty walked up.

"I didn't think you would show up," Martin said as he continued to adjust the cages.

"Had to see what this was all about," Rusty said.

"Just make sure you bet on the right rooster."

"What are you doing?" Rusty asked as Martin kept moving the cages.

"Got to get them even. Don't like it when they aren't even. It's bad luck."

More people arrived and checked their roosters. A crowd began to gather around the pit. They were talking loudly, arguing over which rooster to bet on. Rusty shook his head in amazement. "I never seen so damn many people in the Cove at one time," he said.

"We had more than 500 people at a fight here last year," Martin said. "People said it was the biggest fight they'd ever seen. Biggest fight I'd ever seen."

The man who had taken the money stood up and began making announcements. Martin paid little attention to the proceedings, choosing instead to check his roosters.

"No flat gaffs," the man in the red cap was saying. "No handling the roosters 'til the referee says handle."

The crowd began gathering closer. "Our referee today," the man continued, "is Byron Melton." Melton stepped forward, and the crowd acknowledged his presence.

Out of the Darkness

"Melton is a good referee," Martin explained to Rusty. "Only problem I ever had with him is that he waits too long, sometimes, when the roosters get tangled up before he lets you separate them. He don't take nothing off no one, though."

Rusty nodded, a little unsure what Martin was talking about. Everyone seemed to take the fight seriously. He had imagined it would be a lot less structured, but everything seemed well thought out.

"Remember," the man in the red hat said, "all bets must be made before the handlers loose the roosters in the pit. No welching and no profanity. Any questions?"

No one said anything. "Okay," he said, reaching into a bucket and picking out two slips of paper, "The first match will be between Johnny Bobo's rooster Redman and Bud Parson's second entry Mr. Bojangles. The crowd clapped as the two combatants readied their roosters. A few people tried to make bets, but there was little interest.

"Don't know why Johnny keeps doing this shit," Martin said. "He ain't got a rooster worth a damn, but he always brings one to the fights. Never has won a fight. Hell, he don't even train them."

"All bets in," the man in the red hat said. "You ready, Byron?"

The referee nodded and stepped to the center of the pit.

The two contestants approached the pit from opposite corners. Both held fidgeting roosters under their arms. The tall, broad-shouldered man with a scowl on his face on the right of the pit seemed all business. In the sunlight, his rooster's orange hackle feathers and black tail feathers looked slick, as if they had been coated with oil.

The man on the left, a short, thin man with a large chew of tobacco, talked to the crowd. "Damn good rooster I got here, boys," he said. "Better put some money on him." Most of the crowd shook their heads.

"This won't last long," Martin said.

91

The two men thrust their birds back and forth, beak to beak. The birds became agitated—puffing up, hackles flaring like porcupine quills.

"Last call for bets!" the referee shouted. "Ready! Pit!" The birds exploded from their handlers' grips and smashed together breast to breast. At first, the fight appeared equal, but after about a minute, it was evident that the tall man's rooster would win. The end came quickly. Redman lost his will to fight. He tried to run. The referee called handle. Redman's owner picked him up and tried to force him to return to the fight, but the bird's resolve was broken. After two more failed attempts, the referee declared Mr. Bojangles the winner.

Two more fights took place before Martin's number two rooster, Tabasco, was called. He was pitted against Bud Parson's number one rooster, Thor. "Damn," Martin said when the draw was announced. "I would have to draw Bud the first thing."

"Is that a good rooster?" Rusty asked as Martin removed his rooster from the cage.

"Bud always has good roosters, "Martin said. "That's his best one. Maybe we can wear him down before he gets to Flash."

The betting picked up as spectators sensed this might be one of the better fights. Rusty watched as Martin placed $20.00 on Tabasco.

The fight was intense. The two roosters battled back and forth before Thor caught Tabasco with a shank in the neck. Blood gushed from the wound. Tabasco flopped, tried to stand, but his legs quivered, and he collapsed.

"Damn! Damn! Damn! How the hell did that happened?" Martin said, the words gushing from his lips so rapidly they were barely discernible.

Bud grinned, picked up his rooster, and returned it to its pen. Several people came by to congratulate him.

Martin picked up his rooster and inspected its wounds. The hapless bird flapped around in a feeble attempt to prolong its life as the blood continued to flow from the gash.

"Damn tough break," Rusty said.

"What the hell!" Martin exclaimed, taking the rooster and ringing its neck. He walked over to a large, black, plastic bag and tossed the flopping rooster in.

Several more fights took place, some drawing mild interest from the crowd. Flash won a quick fight against a smallish rooster that seemed more interested in survival. The slip of paper with his name on it went into another jar containing the names of the winners.

After watching several contests, it became obvious to Rusty that Martin and Bud Parson were on a collision course. Though they seemed to respect each other, Rusty guessed that in reality, neither one cared much for the other.

In a much-anticipated match, Flash beat Thor in a hard-fought fight. Both roosters fought valiantly, but with the proficiency of an executioner, Flash trapped Thor in a corner. The two roosters flew at each other. Flash took to the air faster and caught Thor as he was trying to get airborne. Flash slashed Thor's neck, nearly decapitating him.

"Rooster that gets the highest always wins," Martin said. He collected the $400 he had bet. "Told you. You shoulda bet on Flash," he said, waving the cash in his hand.

"Maybe next time," Rusty said.

"D'ju see Flash?"

"Yeah!" Rusty said, a little surprised Flash had won so convincingly.

"Best damn rooster in the Cove. Best damn rooster in the Cove."

The derby, as it was called, wound its way down to the final two contestants: Bud Parson's rooster Mr. Bojangles and Flash. "Here," Martin said, taking all his money out of his pocket and giving it to Lindsey. "We are going to bet it all on Flash."

"Are you sure?" Lindsey asked. "There's more than four hundred dollars there."

"Four hundred forty, to be exact," Martin said.

In less than a minute, he had several takers. Rusty remained quiet, but he could tell that Lindsey didn't like taking a chance of losing all their money.

"Don't worry," Martin said reassuringly. "Flash never loses."

Martin and Bud Parson entered the pit without looking at each other. They pushed the roosters back and forth toward each other, getting them worked up for the fight. At the command to "pit," both roosters crashed into each other, exchanging mid-air kicks. They attacked each other ferociously, beak grabbing beak, hacking wildly with gaff-covered spurs. The crowd was boisterous and excited. Though both roosters were strong, it soon became evident that Flash was much quicker. He slashed Mr. Bojangles from different angles, backing the rooster into the corner. Mr. Bojangles rolled over, apparently suffering a severe injury, and then appeared to revive. Flash was on top of him and they tangled. Bud Parsons grabbed the roosters to separate them. "He can't do that!" Martin shouted as he scrambled to where Parson was untangling the roosters.

"I wuz just getting them loose," Parson said.

"You can't do that until the ref says 'handle.' That's a foul," Martin screamed at the referee.

"Get your rooster!" the referee shouted back.

Martin picked up Flash and noticed a nasty cut on the back of his leg oozing blood. "You cut him, you cheating son of a bitch."

Parson lunged at Martin, but was grabbed before the fight could escalate. Rusty pulled Martin back to his corner. "Damn cheating bastard," Martin kept mumbling.

The roosters resumed fighting. Once again, Flash, though not moving as well as before, began to control the fight. He hacked Mr. Bojangles' legs, and the maimed rooster crumpled in the corner. The crowd cheered.

"Yeah, baby!" Martin shouted.

Flash lunged for the kill. Mr. Bojangles rolled over and Flash impaled himself on Mr. Bojangles' gaff. Flash staggered to the side of the pit; his movements unsteady. Blood poured from his wound, and his breathing sounded like someone in boots walking on gravel.

"Got him in the lung," somebody in the crowd said.

Martin sat there, stunned. Flash crumbled into a heap as Mr. Bojangles struggled to his feet. Flash was counted out.

"Damn, I can't believe he lost," Rusty said.

Martin sat there without speaking. After several minutes, he went and picked up Flash. The rooster was still alive, but its breathing was extremely labored. He gently held him in his arms, carried him to the spring, and tried to get him to drink, but the bird seemed uninterested in the cool, clear water. Rusty followed some distance behind. By the time they got back to Martin's truck, everyone else had gone.

"Where's Lindsey?" Martin asked as he placed Flash in the front seat of his truck.

"Don't know," Rusty lied; he had seen her leave with some guy in a yellow CAT hat.

"The hell with her," Martin said.

Rusty nodded. "You coming to Preacher's tomorrow?" he asked.

"Yeah," Martin said. "I'll be there after the funeral." He stroked Flash's head and drove away.

Chapter 14

Bobby Jack left Preacher's house without telling anyone he was leaving. He had to get home and get his things ready for tomorrow. It looked like it was going to keep raining. He would need something to keep him dry. He had smoked the residue in the pipe at Preacher's house while Preacher was in bed with the two girls. He felt better now. There wasn't much in the pipe, but it was enough to help.

He'd wanted to get it on with that one chick. What was her name? Damn! Maybe it would come to him. He'd look her up later.

He just hadn't been able to get his mind off that pipe. Sex would have been all right. Hell, sex with that chick would probably have been really good. Preacher sure seemed to be enjoying it when both girls were in bed with him. Bobby Jack had been unable to do it. He just couldn't get that damn pipe out of his mind.

That one chick had tried. He wished he could remember her name. She was really built. She was young and definitely willing. He wondered if she thought he was a queer because he couldn't get interested. She had tried. She had really tried. Any other time he would have been game, but he needed that pipe badly. He just couldn't get it out of his mind. He would find her later and show her what kind of a man he was.

Bobby Jack stopped in the road in front of his trailer and looked in his rear view mirror. You couldn't be too careful with all the things going on now. Last week, a cop car had been driving around the Cove, so he had to be on the lookout.

Crushed beer cans overflowed a box on his porch. He had been keeping them in a box to sell, but the rain had caused the box to fall apart, and now the cans were scattered everywhere. The yard was littered with wadded McDonald's sacks, candy wrappers, and Cracker Jack boxes.

Bobby Jack looked at his gas gauge before turning the key. He had half a tank. There was no use driving to Booneville just to get two dollars worth of gas. That was all the money he had, and with prices the way they were, that wouldn't even get him a gallon. Preacher said gas and everything else went up because of the war. "Another Vietnam," was what Preacher called it.

Bobby Jack got the two boxes he found in the barn out of his truck. He unlocked the padlock on his door and carried them inside. The clothes on the top of the first box were wet from the rain, and Bobby Jack tossed them to the floor with the assortment of other clothes already lying there. He continued to dig through the box, discarding most of the items without much notice. There were several old sweaters and a dress that looked like it might have been worn to a prom.

The next item attracted his interest. It was small, no more than two feet by one foot and bright red. It looked as if it had been folded with great care. Bobby Jack picked it up by the corners, and it fell open. "Damn," he said aloud as he inspected the Nazi flag.

The black swastika reeked with evil. Maybe Mr. Furness really had been a Nazi. The stories his brothers told him could be true. Bobby Jack traced the design with his fingers. The material was heavy, and the swastika was sewn on with heavy black thread. He held it in his hand for a long time and tried to imagine the things that had happened underneath that banner. He folded the flag and put it on his head like a doo-rag.

Underneath the flag was an old wooden box. Bobby Jack raised the lid. The rusty hinges creaked. A belt with a silver buckle glistened in the light. Bobby Jack tried to make out the word—GOTTMITUNS. The letters were all in capital and underneath was an eagle with a Nazi swastika in its talons. Bobby Jack had no idea what it meant, but he was sure it was something German. He might go in to Booneville later and find out.

Bobby Jack stood up and removed his belt. It was well worn and several holes had been punched in it with a nail to accommodate the weight he had lost. He put on the new belt and fastened the prongs. He walked to the mirror and admired his find.

He went through the rest of the box. In the bottom, Bobby Jack spied a stack of newspaper clippings. They were yellow and faded. He picked one up. The brittle paper nearly crumbled in his hands. He unfolded it with care, trying not to tear the edges.

"War Criminals Sought," the article said in bold letters. It was dated March 3, 1946. Bobby Jack had difficulty reading it, but he made out the names of Martin Borman and Josef Mengele, two of the most notorious war criminals missing from the Nuremberg Trials. The rest of the article was a jumble of letters Bobby Jack found too complicated to understand.

Several articles were written in German. Bobby Jack was unable to understand the writing, but the pictures were very clear. In one, Hitler was speaking before a large crowd of soldiers. They all had their hands raised in salute. Bobby Jack made the familiar raised-hand salute at the mirror on his wall.

A knock on the door brought him back from his daydream. *Who would be knocking on his door? What could they want?* He took the boxes and put them in the bedroom, and he went to a drawer and got out a pistol. "Who is it?"

"It's me," Dennis said. "Hurry up and let me in."

Bobby Jack opened the door. Rain was coming down hard, blowing in sheets against the side of the trailer. As soon as the door opened, Dennis stepped inside and shook the rain from his hair.

"What the hell are you doing?"

"My mother fell. I think she may have broken something," he said between heavy breaths. "My truck is out of gas. I need a gallon to get her to the doctor."

Bobby Jack thought for a minute. "I ain't got no gas."

"Damn, I gotta find something. She might be hurt bad."

"Take my truck."

"You sure?"

"Yeah, I ain't gonna need it tonight," Bobby Jack said, handing Dennis the keys.

"I don't think I can get her in that thing the way it's jacked up," Dennis said, shaking his head.

"Tell you what," Bobby Jack said. "I got a half-tank of gas. We'll go back to your house and siphon some out of my tank into yours."

"You sure?"

"Yeah."

"Thanks," Dennis said. "I didn't know what I was going to do."

"No problem." Bobby Jack got his coat.

Dennis climbed in the passenger's side. He felt high enough to be in an airplane. "You got a hose?"

"Always prepared," Bobby Jack said, reaching behind the seat and bringing out a five-foot section of hosepipe.

It was a short drive to Dennis' house. The rain still beat down, and thunder reverberated throughout the valley. It didn't appear that the downpour was going to let up. Bobby Jack backed into the driveway next to Dennis's truck. Within seconds, he had gas flowing into the empty vehicle.

"Let me help you with your mother," Bobby Jack said after he finished with the gas.

"It might be hard to do it by myself," Dennis admitted.

They walked into the house. Dennis's mother was still lying on the floor. Dennis had placed a handmade quilt over her to keep her warm. She had a pillow under her head and appeared to be asleep.

"Ma, we are going to take you to the doctor."

"Where's Henry? I can't go without Henry."

"He'll be along in a minute," Bobby Jack said, trying to calm her.

"Who are you?" she asked with indignation.

"Bobby Jack Morris."

"Are you Eliza's boy?"

"No, I'm John Morris's youngest boy."

"John Morris ain't nothing but a horse thief."

"Yes, ma'am, I expect that's about right."

"You ain't a horse thief, are you?"

"Ma, leave Bobby Jack alone. He's here to help."

Bobby Jack winked at Dennis. "It's okay. I don't reckon I ever stole a horse," he said.

"Well, that's a good thing. You know they hang horse thieves."

"I expect that's true," Bobby Jack said.

They slid a blanket underneath her and carried her to the truck. They put her inside, leaned her back, and closed the door.

"Thanks for everything," Dennis said.

"No problem. You need me to go with you to the emergency room?"

Dennis shook his head. "I got it from here. I owe you one."

Bobby Jack nodded and watched Dennis's lights disappear into the driving rain.

Chapter 15

Shelby dressed Nicole in a light pink sweat suit and carried her to the car. She placed her hand on Nicole's forehead. The child was still warm. When she had taken her temperature earlier in the morning, it had been 103 degrees.

"Dr. Spangler will make you feel better, sweetie," Shelby said. The little girl didn't respond. "He will give you some medicine, and you will be up and playing in no time."

"Mama, will I have to get a shot?" Nicole asked.

"Probably not," Shelby said.

"Good! I hate shots. They hurt."

"It will be okay, honey," Shelby assured her.

She buckled Nicole in her car seat and strapped her in snugly. The silver Nissan Sentra cranked on the third try. She sighed in relief. Two days ago, at her parent's house, she had been forced to use the jumper cables when the engine wouldn't turn over.

It was beginning to rain. Her wipers didn't work well, smearing the windshield and making it harder to see. She was in a hurry, but drove slowly down the twisting road that led to Booneville.

Shelby pulled up to the brown brick building that housed Doctors Spangler and Kennedy. Though the building was old, it had been landscaped. Azaleas lined the front of the building, interspersed with strategically placed holly trees. Variegated monkey grass edged both sides of the walkway to the front steps.

Several cars were in the parking lot. When she had spoken with the receptionist this morning, neither doctor had an opening, but because Nicole was so sick, they agreed to work her in.

The office was crowded. The receptionist, a chubby brunette, handed Shelby a paper to fill out and told her to sign the register book. After completing the paperwork, Shelby and Nicole sat in one of the few empty seats in the waiting room.

"Hello, there," a familiar voice said.

"Hi, Gary," Shelby said, surprised. "I didn't even see you sitting there."

"I didn't think I was that tiny," Gary said.

Shelby laughed. At 6'4" and 250lbs, no one would ever accuse Gary Simms of being small.

"Who's this pretty little girl?" Gary asked.

"This is Nicole. Can you say hello to Gary?" Shelby asked.

"Hi," she said her voice barely above a whisper.

"You are a mighty pretty girl," Gary said, "and you have the most beautiful brown eyes I have ever seen."

Nicole hugged her mother tightly.

"She isn't feeling well. I think she may have the flu. Several people I know have had it," Shelby said.

"I think it's going around," Gary agreed.

"How old are you, Nicole?" Gary asked.

Nicole held up four fingers.

"Can't you tell Gary how old you are?" Shelby asked.

Nicole shook her head.

"So, Gary, what have you been up to?"

"Just the usual—work, work, work."

"That doesn't sound like the Gary I remember," Shelby countered.

"Well, maybe I did exaggerate a little," Gary confessed.

"How's Jake?" Shelby asked, looking around to see if anyone was listening. Everyone seemed engrossed in his or her own business—reading, talking, or too sick to care.

"He's doing well. I don't see him that much, even though we live practically next door to each other—mostly at family outings and that type of thing. Aunt Eve always wants me to bring Mom and Dad over for dinner."

"She always did love to cook," Shelby said, recalling Sunday dinners at the Patton's.

"Have you seen his house?" Gary asked.

Shelby shook her head no, even though she had driven by it a couple times.

"It makes my place look like Green Acres," Gary said.

"I'm sure you have a nice place, too," Shelby said.

"Jake has been working on another book for some time now. I'm not sure how it is going. He is real secretive about that stuff," Gary said.

"What's this one about?" Shelby asked.

"Did you read *Artic Fire?*" Gary asked.

"No," Shelby said, "but I heard it was good."

"It was good—a lot different than anything I ever expected Jake to write. It's got a lot of action in it, but it also has a lot of symbolism and philosophy."

"What about the book he's writing now?" Shelby asked.

"Well, this book is nothing like *Artic Fire*. As far as I know, it doesn't have a name, but I do know it has a Civil War background," Gary said.

"No such thing as a civil war," Shelby said. "At least that is what Jake always used to say."

"Yeah," Gary said. "I have heard that a bunch of times myself. That's something he picked up from Andrew Lytle. Did you ever meet him?"

"Jake took me to his log cabin in Monteagle several times when we were dating."

"Mr. Lytle always called the Civil War the War of the Northern Invasion. Jake adopted that from him," Gary said. "I prefer to call it the War Between the States, myself."

"Mr. Lytle was a fascinating man," Shelby said. "He and Jake would talk history and writing for hours. Most of it was over my head."

"Yeah," Gary said. "Mine, too. You know it was Mr. Lytle that convinced Jake to go to Vanderbilt."

"I always thought Jake would go to Ole Miss. I remember how much he loved the campus when he went there on a recruiting trip."

"Mr. Lytle was a Vanderbilt alumnus, and he encouraged Jake to give it a chance," Gary said. "Lytle was a member of a group of Vanderbilt students and alumni, called the Agrarians."

"As I recall, they wrote a famous book—I can't think of the name of it," Shelby said, trying to remember the name she had heard so often over the years.

"*I'll Take My Stand.*"

"*I'll Take My Stand.* That's it. I can't believe I forgot it," Shelby said, relieved to know the name. "I remember Jake and Mr. Lytle talking about it all the time."

"You know Mr. Lytle died a couple years back," Gary said.

"I read it in the paper. I didn't know he was so well known," Shelby replied, "but the newspapers were full of stories about his life and accomplishments."

"Jake was upset after it happened. He had just got over his knee surgery, and then the man he thought of as his grandfather died. It was hard on him. He took several months and went out west to clear his head."

"What did he do out there by himself?" Shelby asked.

"He kayaked a lot, did some mountain climbing and a lot of soul searching, I guess," Gary said.

"Is Jake dating anyone?" Shelby asked.

"No one steady, as far as I know," Gary said.

"I saw his picture in the paper at a book signing with someone," Shelby said.

"His agent is always trying to get his picture in the paper. I don't think it was anyone he was involved with."

"I don't know," Shelby said. "She was pretty."

Gary shook his head. "What has been going on with you?" he asked.

"Just the normal stuff," she said. "Keeping up with a four-year-old is a full-time job."

"What happened to you?" Gary asked, noting the bruises on her face and her swollen and sore lip.

"I fell down the steps," Shelby said, looking down at the worn green carpet. "You know how clumsy I am."

"Shelby, you don't have to live like that—"

"No! Really," Shelby interrupted. "I fell down the steps."

"Shelby—"

"Nicole," the nurse said. "You all come on back."

"It was nice to talk to you, Gary," Shelby said.

"If there is ever anything I can do, and I mean anything, just let me know," Gary said.

"Thanks," she said, squeezing his arm.

When she turned to leave, Preacher Bess was standing behind her. "Good morning, Shelby," he said. "I see you are conversing with our local war hero."

Shelby smiled halfheartedly.

"Hello, Simms," Preacher said.

Shelby picked up Nicole and went into the examining room.

"I didn't see you slither in, Arthur," Gary said.

Preacher ignored the insult. "How's the family?" he asked as he picked up a red Gideon Bible and thumbed through the pages.

"Like you care," Gary said, obviously irritated.

"That's no way to talk to kinfolk," Preacher said. "We need to let bygones be bygones."

"You and I aren't any kin."

"We're all kin from Adam."

"We are no kin at all, Preacher."

"Well you are kin to the Pattons, and so am I," Preacher said. "I guess that makes us family."

"As I recall," Gary said, "you swore you would get even with my family if it was the last thing you ever did."

"All that stuff I said was just because I was young and foolish. I was mad at Ben Patton. He stole my mama's land, and you know it," Preacher said.

"That's crazy talk," Gary said. "Ben never stole that land. He gave your mother ten times what it was worth just to help her out."

"Oh yeah! He helped her out, all right. Just how much money did you all make off those bluff lots?" Preacher asked.

"When Ben bought that mountain land from your mother, it was selling everywhere for fifty dollars an acre and good farm land sold for a thousand dollars or less an acre. Ben paid her $50,000 for land worth only $5,000 or $6,000."

"But then y'all sold one acre and made the $50,000 back," Preacher said.

"That was twenty years later. No one knew at the time Ben bought it how valuable bluff property would become," Gary said.

"Well, it's over with and forgotten," Preacher said. "What are you here for?"

"I got this sinus mess and can't get rid of it," Gary said defensively.

"Ever since that chopper went down in Vietnam, I've had this back trouble. I haven't had a day without pain since," Preacher said.

"A lot of people have pain from that war," Gary said looking at the scars on his arm from a bullet he took near Da Nang.

"Mr. Simms," the nurse said.

"Watch yourself, Arthur," Gary said.

"You ain't in Nam' any more, Sarge, so maybe you better watch yourself," Preacher said.

"Just what is your problem?" Gary asked, loud enough that everyone in the waiting room looked up to see what was going on.

"My problem? My problem? See this?" he said, rolling up his sleeves to reveal scars on his hands and arms. "I get shot down in a chopper, almost break my back, nearly burn alive, see my buddies die in the fire, and all I get for my effort is unbearable pain in my back every time I take a step. You shoot a couple Charlies and toss a couple grenades, and you get a promotion and a chest full of metals. No, I can't imagine what my problem could be."

"Preacher, you are pitiful. You have no idea what went on. I feel sorry for you. You're pathetic."

"You are the one that better watch yourself," Preacher said.

Chapter 16

Martin opened the door and sunlight bathed the darkened interior of the trailer. The inside smelled of piss, and Martin made a face as he walked into the kitchen. Renee looked up from where she was sitting on the floor and shaded her eyes from the light.

"What the hell are ya'll doing?" Martin asked.

"Billy has got some stuff for us to do one," Renee said.

"Why you got all the lights off? You need more than that flashlight to see by."

Renee got up and turned on the lights. "We thought we saw somebody outside. A white car kept driving by. We thought it might be the cops."

"That was just Mrs. Mantooth," Martin said. "Ya'll are going to blow yourselves up trying to do this in the dark."

Billy Gladhill and a girl with a butch-looking haircut squinted in the brightness. Billy was always hanging around, but Martin didn't recognize the girl. She had a washed-out look. Her skin looked as if it hadn't seen the sun in years, and her cheeks and eyes were sunken and hollow.

Billy stood up; his hair was long and matted. "We'd give you some if you'd cook it for us."

"I ain't got time now. I got things to do, but I'll be back in a couple hours or so. I'll cook it then if you want."

No one said anything. Martin looked around, thinking they hadn't heard him.

Finally, the girl spoke. Her voice was coarse and grating. "We need it before then."

"Who are you?" Martin asked.

"Penny Hobbs," she said, half-smiling.

"Where you from?"

"Originally from Tullahoma. Been living around here for a while."

Martin closed the door, went to the sink, and washed his hands. "Damn, it stinks in here. Don't any of you take a bath?"

Billy shrugged his shoulders. "You know how it is when you are on it. Taking a bath gets it out of your system quicker."

"Hell, you all look like you have already come down. Least you could do is wash your clothes."

"Don't pay no attention to Martin," Renee said. "He takes three or four showers a day. He's scared of germs."

"Least I don't smell like three-day-old piss."

"We'll clean up when we get this stuff cooking," the girl said.

"We got a bunch of stuff," Billy said pointing to the two garbage bags on the floor.

"Where'd you get all this?" Martin asked.

"Don't matter none where we got it," Billy said, crossing his arms and looking directly at Martin. "Thing is that we got it, and you could have some of it."

"You ever cooked any before?" Martin asked.

Billy hesitated. The only time he had tried, he had started a fire that burned down an old, abandoned house. He had been lucky not to get burned himself. "No, but I've seen it done."

"Well, it's real easy to mess up a batch, and it's even easier to blow the whole damn thing up," Martin said.

"That's why we'd like you to do the cooking," Billy said.

"Tell you what I'll do," Martin said. "I'll tell you what to do for half the stuff."

"Half of what we cook?" Billy asked.

"Naw," Martin said. "Half of everything you got to make it."

Billy looked at the two girls, who were staring wide-eyed back at him. He rubbed the fuzz on his chin as he thought about the offer. "Can't do it."

"Okay," Martin said. "Cook it yourself, but not in my trailer."

"It's my trailer, too," Renee said, her voice rising to a squeaky high.

"Who the hell is paying for it?" Martin yelled. "When have you ever paid for anything? Do you ever even pay the electric bill? What little money the government gives you ain't enough to even pay for what your kids need."

"It helps," she protested.

"It helps that our mother raises them while you're out being a crank whore."

"Just what do you think you are—a damn school teacher or something?"

"No, but I take care of my business, and nobody screws with me."

"We don't need you anyway, you asshole," Renee shouted.

"Make the shit yourself," Martin said. He turned and walked down the narrow hall to his bedroom.

A large waterbed occupied a major portion of the small bedroom. Clothes were neatly hung in the bedroom closet. An iron sat on the dresser top; its cord wound carefully around it. A bottle of Stetson and several cans of deodorant sat next to it. Martin got a towel and went to bathroom.

After he showered, he put on a black AC/DC shirt and a pair of black jeans. He straightened up the cans of deodorant on the dresser and rearranged the pillows on his bed before returning to the living room.

The living room floor was covered with batteries. Penny sat on the floor, removing them from their packages. "We've talked about it," Billy said. "You can have half the stuff if you'll teach us how to cook it."

Martin looked in the black garbage bags. "Empty everything on the floor," he said.

Billy and Renee dumped the remaining contents on the floor. "Okay," Martin said, taking control like a professor in a classroom. "First thing you need to do is remove the casings from these batteries and get the strips. Before you do that, put mine in this bag."

Billy picked up a several hands full and tossed them in the bag. "That enough?" he asked.

"Yeah," Martin said. "Renee, open up them boxes of Tylenol Sinus and get all the pills out. Don't forget my half."

While they were getting things ready, he went outside to the building behind the trailer. He moved the lawn mower out of the way and got a five-gallon bucket and a rubber hose.

Back inside, he picked up a gallon of ammonia and poured it in the bucket. "How many of these you got?" he asked.

"Eight," Penny said.

"You only need about three," he said, pouring the remaining amount in the bucket. "I'll take the rest." He put the pills and the lithium strips in the bucket with the ammonia.

"Got any starter fluid?"

They all shook their head. "Do we have to have that?" Billy asked.

"It helps, but we can make do without it. Renee, get under the sink and get me that bottle of Draino. While you are there, get me that glass bottle under the sink, too, and some aluminum foil."

Martin watched the others as Renee got what they needed. Billy was staring intently at what Martin was doing, trying to remember how to do it. He was so burned out that Martin doubted he would ever be able to do it without killing himself. Penny was getting antsy. He could tell by the way she fidgeted that she was getting excited. Watching her aroused him. Maybe sometime, when he didn't have so much to do, he'd see what this skinny little girl could do for him.

Renee brought the things he asked for and sat them on the table. He took a bottle of sulfuric acid and poured half of it in the glass bottle. "Better be damn careful with this shit," he said. "It will eat you to the bone."

The others watched intently as he wadded up a ball of aluminum foil and placed it in the bottle. He put one end of the hose in the mouth of the bottle and wrapped it with more of the aluminum foil. He took the free end of the hose and placed it in the bucket.

"When it stops bubbling," Martin said, "stir it and let it sit for at least three or four hours."

"Is that it?" Billy asked.

"Yeah, and don't piss in it."

Billy looked sheepish, as Martin kept talking.

"After it sits for a while, there is going to be all kinds of nasty liquid on top. Pour the liquid off. You'll see a gunk of stuff at the bottom. That's the meth. Get it out and let it dry."

"Hey, man, thanks," Billy said. "We can handle it from here."

"You'll probably want to crush it to make crank. Crush it up real fine, and it will go further than ice."

"Uhhhh, ice," Penny said. "It makes you soar."

"Well there ain't gonna be too much," Martin said, "but you can divide it up anyway you want. Keep that fire low and don't mix anything else in it while it's cooking, or you'll blow the whole damn house up." He slung his garbage bag over his shoulder, opened the door, and walked outside. The sky was overcast, but a few rays of sunshine streaked through the gray clouds.

Chapter 17

Shelby left the doctor's office and drove to a small store two blocks away. She parked in front of a red brick building. "Do you feel like going inside with Mommy?" she asked.

"Uh-huh," Nicole said, excited. "Where are we?"

"It's a book and hobby shop. I have a friend who works here that I haven't seen in a long time. I just want to go inside and say hello."

"Okay."

"When we get inside you have to be good for Mommy, okay?"

"Okay."

"Don't be getting things off the shelves."

"Okay, Mommy."

The bell on the door jingled as they opened it and went inside.

"Well, well. Hello, Miss Shelby. I haven't seen you in a while."

"It has been a long time, Mr. Gray."

Who is this young lady with you?"

"This is Nicole. She's been a little under the weather, so we went to see Dr. Spangler."

"Hi there, sweetie, how are you?"

"Good," Nicole said, burying her head against her mother's leg.

"She is pretty shy about talking to people," Shelby explained, "but we are working on that."

"She is a mighty pretty young lady."

"It has been a while, Mr. Gray. How have you been?"

"Just getting older and fatter," he said, rubbing his hands through his thinning white hair and patting his round stomach. "How about you?"

"Staying busy. Having a child is a full-time job."

"Well, I am glad you stopped in. Is there anything I can help you with?"

"I'm just looking around."

"I was afraid you had stopped painting,"

"I haven't painted anything in a long time."

"That's a shame. You are so good."

Shelby laughed. "I think you must have me confused with someone else."

"Remember this?" he asked, pointing to a painting hanging on the wall. It appeared to be an Impressionist view of the banks of a lake.

"I can't believe you still have this."

"I have been around art for over forty years. I know a good artist when I see one. You are very good. I expect this to be worth lots of money one day."

"I doubt that," Shelby said.

"Why don't you start painting again?"

"I might someday. I am not even sure I still have a brush."

"I got stuff everywhere. Take what you want."

"I don't have much money."

"You don't need money here. I'll take your first painting as full payment."

"I think you are getting the short end of the stick."

"You let me worry about that."

"Thanks."

The store was packed with various art supplies. She picked up two canvasses, three small tubes of paint, and a small brush.

"That's not enough," Mr. Gray said. He filled a sack with painting supplies and handed it to her.

"Oh! Mr. Gray, I couldn't take all this—"

"Hush. Get out of here and take care of that pretty little girl."

"Thank you," Shelby said, giving him a hug.

"I'm expecting a painting in two weeks," Mr. Gray said with a chuckle.

The sound of the door caused her to turn. She couldn't believe it. *What was he doing here?*

"Hello, Jake," Mr. Gray said to Jake Patton as he opened the door and came inside.

"Hi, Mr. Gray," Jake said in a very animated voice.

Shelby's back was to Jake, and she wasn't sure he had seen her. She took Nicole's hand and led her down the nearest aisle.

"Where are we going?" Nicole asked.

"Look for a book while Mommy does something," she said, moving to where she could see what was going on up front.

At the end of the aisle where she stopped was a book display featuring a large poster of *Artic Fire* along with a picture of Jake. Mr. Gray was talking to Jake about a book signing. Shelby eased to the opposite side of the store, near the door. She could just walk out, but she couldn't leave without telling Mr. Gray good-bye. Maybe Jake would leave soon. She wanted to see Jake, and yet she was afraid to see him. She wasn't sure what she was afraid of. Maybe she was afraid of stirring up old feelings. Maybe she was afraid it wouldn't stir them. She couldn't take that chance. Rusty would kill her if he found out she had talked to Jake. She would just pick up Nicole and walk out the door. She would yell goodbye to Mr. Gray. Jake wouldn't follow her.

Where was Nicole? She had been there just a second ago. Shelby started to panic. "Looks like you got another fan," she heard Mr. Gray say.

She saw Jake and Mr. Gray walk toward the back of the store, near where she was. She retraced her steps, and there was Nicole, staring at the life-size picture of Jake Patton. She waited as the two men approached. "What do you think of this poster?" Mr. Gray asked.

"It's big!" Nicole said, still staring at the poster.

"Do you know who that is?" Mr. Gray asked.

"Nope," she said.

"That's a famous author," Mr. Gray said.

"Don't you listen to him, honey," Jake said. "It's just a poster of a guy that happened to write a book."

"He sure is big. What's his name?"

"Do you recognize this fellow?" Mr. Gray asked, pointing to Jake.

Nicole turned and looked at Jake. "You're the guy in the poster," she said in amazement.

"My name's Jake Patton. What's yours?"

"Nicole Leigh Miller."

"Well, Nicole Leigh Miller, it is a pleasure to meet you."

"Do you know my mommy, too?"

"I'm not sure," Jake began. "I've been out of town a lot lately, and I don't—" He stopped mid-sentence. She walked from behind a row of books, and a flood of memories returned. "Shelby?"

"Hi, Jake," was all she could mutter, her voice trembling.

"Is this your daughter?"

She almost couldn't speak. It was so difficult. She took a deep breath and hesitated for minutes before she managed to say, "Yes."

"She is absolutely darling," Mr. Gray interjected.

"She certainly is," Jake concurred.

"Look at those gorgeous brown eyes," Mr. Gray continued. "She's a doll."

"Just how old are you?" Jake asked.

Nicole held up four fingers, but continued to look at the poster and then Jake.

"She is fascinated with this poster of you. You seem to have that effect on women," Shelby said.

Jake was a little unsure how to answer. Mr. Gray sensed the tension and interrupted. "How about you and I go get a Coke, if that's okay with your mom?"

Shelby was hesitant. "We need to go," she said.

"Please, Mommy!"

"I've got a machine right up front," Mr. Gray said.

"Well, okay, but just for a minute." Nicole hurried off hand in hand with Mr. Gray.

Mr. Gray is a wonderful man," Jake said.

"Yeah, he's the best."

There was a moment of awkward silence. Then they both spoke at the same time and laughed at their gaffe. "Okay," Jake said. "Let's try this again."

Shelby smiled. Jake always loved her smile. "So, how have you been?" he asked.

"Okay. Chasing around after Nicole keeps me busy."

"She is gorgeous. She looks just like you."

Shelby shook her head, and for the first time looked directly into Jake's coffee-colored eyes. She felt lightheaded. She struggled to maintain control, feeling like she was back in high school. "I don't have brown eyes," she said, her voice quivering.

"Well, there's no mistaking that beautiful smile."

"Looks like you made it big-time," Shelby said, pointing to the poster and the numerous copies of *Artic Fire* on the racks.

"Have you read it?"

"No, but I hear it is really good."

"The critics seem to like it, but it hasn't sold as well as I had hoped."

"It seems to be doing fine from what I've been told."

Jake shrugged his shoulders. His modesty had endured him to her. "Would you like a copy?" he asked.

Shelby stared at the floor. "No, I better not," she said.

"Why?"

"I just don't think it's a good idea."

Jake sensed this was his opportunity to make up for all the things he wished he had said and done in the past. He knew he could spend a lifetime looking for and not finding anyone like Shelby. He had been foolish and lost her. Now he wanted to explain his actions to her.

His parents had only wanted what was best for him. Go to school and get an education. How many times had he heard his father preach that? What an opportunity he had to play football in the Southeastern Conference. A degree from Vanderbilt was the carrot dangling at the end of the string.

He should have made things clear to Shelby, but he could never find the right words. She thought his parents didn't like her, that they didn't think she was good enough for him. Her parents were decent, hard-working people, and neither Ben nor Eve had ever had anything bad to say about them. But Shelby had assumed it had something to do with the different social status. He had tried to rationalize his actions. Why had he been so indecisive? He was always indecisive. It was too late to change things, but he needed her to know the truth.

"Shelby, I am really sorry about—"

"How's your mom?" Shelby said, interrupting him before he had a chance to continue.

"She and Dad are both fine. They just seem to keep going. I don't think they will ever quit work."

"That's probably good. Work will keep them young."

"Shelby, what I was trying to say was that—"

"So, are you seeing anybody?"

"No, not really. I'm too busy working on my book."

"How's that going?"

"Shelby, there is something I really want to talk to you about."

"Jake, don't. That's past history, and didn't you once tell me that history is just a fable that people agree on?"

"I can't believe you remember me saying that."

"I remember everything you told me. I remember that you told me how you went to the barn and sat on bales of hay and cried for hours the night your grandmother died. I remember you told me you would always love me."

"Shelby, I—"

"I remember everything about us, Jake, but most of all, I remember how painful it was when you broke up with me."

"Shelby, I am sorry about that. I would give anything if I could change it."

"Jake, I—"

"Shelby, I still care about you."

She chuckled in disbelief. *Why would he say he cared?* "Is that why you broke my heart?" she asked.

"Do you remember the weekend after we broke up? I called you, and we went for a walk to Stone Door. It was a warm spring day. The trees were budding all over the mountain. It was a perfect day, and then it started to rain."

"Of course, I remember. We were drenched by the time we got to Stone Door and found a dry place underneath a large boulder."

"I tried to talk to you that day. I tried to explain my actions, but you wouldn't listen to me."

"What was there to explain? You didn't want me any more."

"That's not true."

"It sure seemed that way from my point of view."

"I want to explain now."

"It's too late now, Jake, way too late."

"Shelby, I am worried about you."

"Now is a really good time to start worrying about my feelings."

"I saw Carrie at Wal-Mart. She told me you and Rusty were having problems."

"Nothing I can't handle."

"What about those bruises on your face?" he said, brushing her hair back to reveal a dark bruise on her cheekbone, only partially covered with makeup. When his hand touched her face, she felt a rush of blood, and goose bumps covered her body. Why did he always do that to her?

"I fell," she said, regaining some of her composure.

"And the busted lip?"

"It all happened when I fell off the steps."

"Sure."

"Jake, just stay out of my life. I loved you with all my heart and still—"

"Mommy! Mommy! Look what Mr. Gray gave me," Nicole said as she ran to Shelby. She proudly held up a bottle of Sundrop and took a gulp.

"I hope you don't mind," Mr. Gray said. "I know it is loaded with caffeine, but it was what she said she wanted."

"It will be fine," Shelby assured him.

"Look what else I got," Nicole said, holding up a child's paint set.

"Mr. Gray, you shouldn't keep giving us stuff," Shelby said.

"I just look at it like I am sponsoring an artist and possibly a future artist," he said.

"Are you still painting?" Jake asked Shelby.

"I haven't painted anything in a long time, but I am thinking about starting again."

"You should. You were very good, wasn't she, Mr. Gray?"

"'I told her that I have been in this business a long time, and she is the best I have ever known in person."

"You two are going to give me a big head."

"Daddy said if I didn't listen to him he'd thump my head—"

"Nicole, we better get going," Shelby said, eager to change the subject.

"Take care," Mr. Gray said, patting Nicole on the head, "and be sure to bring this young lady back for a visit."

"Bye, Mr. Gray," Nicole said, extending her hand.

Mr. Gray shook her hand. "Bye," he said with a wink.

"Goodbye, Mr. Jake."

"Goodbye, Nicole," Jake said, wising he could prolong the encounter. "It has been a pleasure meeting you."

Shelby fastened Nicole in her car seat, got in, and started the car. As she started out of the parking lot, someone in an old truck waved at her. At first, she didn't recognize who it was, but on closer inspection, there was no doubt. Preacher Bess grinned and waved as she drove by where his truck was sitting. Was he following her, she wondered.

Chapter 18

After Shelby and Nicole had gone, Mr. Gray took off his glasses and pulled an old white handkerchief out of his back pocket. He rubbed the smudges and held the glasses up to the light to see if they were clean. "Do you think she is okay?" he asked.

"I don't know," Jake said. "I've heard all kinds of stories."

Mr. Gray bent over and straightened up some books that had been put back in the wrong place. "She had a black eye," he said.

"I asked her about it, and she said she fell."

"She's got a cut lip, too."

"She said that happened at the same time," Jake said.

"It looked like she was hit to me."

"Yeah, me, too."

"Somebody needs to do something. She's such a fine young lady."

"What could anybody do?" Jake asked. "He's her husband."

"That doesn't give him the right to hit her."

"No, but she needs to be the one to get out of that situation."

"My guess is she's scared."

Mr. Gray continues straightening the books on the shelves. Jake picked up a copy of *Artic Fire* and thumbed through it without really looking at the pages.

He had tried to rationalize things in his mind. He was going away to college. They were too young to get married. He had always envisioned that someday they would get married. In his dreams, she was always there, waiting on him, when he graduated from college.

His parents had been so insistent on him going to school. He should have stood up to them, told them how he felt. He had gambled and lost. Not only had he lost Shelby, he had lost himself.

"I don't know, Mr. Gray," he heard himself say aloud. "I just don't know what to do."

Mr. Gray shook his head. "Youth is a blunder, adulthood a struggle, and old age a regret," he said. "I have too many regrets. I hope you overcome your blunders before you, too, have a load of regrets."

"Mr. Gray, life is just too complicated."

Jake and Mr. Gray said goodbye. Jake walked outside. The rain had slacked and rays of sunshine were trying to poke through the gray sky. Next to Jake's Toyota Tundra sat an older model two-tone blue truck. It was backed into the parking space, and Jake noticed that its back bumper had been damaged and the taillight was broken.

"Good afternoon, Mr. Patton," Preacher said. He rested both arms on the driver's side window and smiled at Jake. His arms were wiry. The menacing head of a cobra covered one forearm, and equally menacing scars covered the other.

"What's this 'Mr. Patton' stuff, Arthur?" Jake asked.

"No, sir," Preacher said, his voice dragging out every syllable. "A man's gotta respect his betters."

Jake shook his head and opened the door to his truck. Preacher had parked so close there was barely enough room. "I hear you made it big with that book you wrote," Preacher said.

Jake stared at Preacher's implacable face, unsure of where Preacher was going with his comments. *Was he trying to make him say or do something he would regret?* "It's done okay," he said.

"What the hell does a pussy boy like you know about war?" Preacher said, his voice rising.

Jake's face reddened. He took a deep breath, closed the door of his truck, and turned to face Preacher. "You got a problem with my book, or is the problem with me?"

"Onliest problem I got is I don't know how in the hell you can write about something you know nothing about."

"Just because I wasn't in the army—"

"Just because of your name."

"My name's got nothing to do with it. I've read everything I could find about WWII."

"Guess being a Patton makes you an expert on everything. You Pattons have some special gift the rest of us common folks don't got."

"It's fiction—"

"I've been there! I know what it's like to have people shoot at your ass and try to—"

"It's fiction!" Jake yelled.

"I guess you got the Midas touch, too."

"What?"

"Ben Patton wouldn't have that horse or nothing if he hadn't stole it."

Jake grabbed Preacher by the collar. He wanted to yank him out of the truck and pummel his face. His mother's words kept ringing in his ear. *He's had a rough life; you have to overlook some of the things he does. There's good in everybody if you look deep enough.*

When his mother died, Preacher became angry with Ben even though he had paid Mary's hospital bill. Ben gave her family money to live on, and when she died, Ben paid the funeral bill. Every time Ben gave Mary money for food and medicine, he suspected she gave part of it to Preacher. She had always been that way. The thing that really aggravated Ben was that when she died, Preacher told everyone that would listen that Ben had cheated her out of money and disowned her. Ben had wanted to confront Preacher, "take him to the woodshed," but Eve had stopped him.

"He hasn't had much of a chance in life," Eve had said. "Mary did the best she could, but it's hard to raise a boy alone, and she was sick a lot."

"I'm not too sure it's his raising," Ben said. "It looks to me more like it is bad genes."

"He's harmless, Ben," she said, not willing to concede that Ben was right. "Besides, everyone knows you took care of Mary."

"To think he'd have the gall to say I cheated my own sister makes me want to smack him in the mouth."

"Violence never solves anything," Eve said. "It only creates more violence."

The incident irritated Ben, like a splinter just beneath the skin. He never fully agreed with Eve, but had deferred to her wishes. Outwardly, he ignored Preacher's insults. Inwardly, he simmered, but Eve's calm kept matters from boiling over until the previous year.

Every Fourth of July, the community celebrated Independence Day with a picnic and parade. Several local people, including Ben, rode horses in the parade. The procession ended at the school, and most of the people gathered along the route near there. As they approached the school, Preacher staggered from a group of men, cussing Ben and waving his arms. Ben's horse was startled by the abrupt action and reared. Ben had managed to stay mounted, but Amy King, Ben's ten-year-old, neighbor was thrown from her pony.

Ben dismounted and ran to check on Amy. She was uninjured, except for her pride. Ben was irate. He marched to where Preacher was standing. Preacher was startled to see Ben in such a rage.

"You damn drunken fool!" Ben shouted. "You could have got someone killed."

Preacher stammered, trying to explain. Before he could answer, Ben landed a solid right fist on his chin. Preacher sprawled to the pavement.

Though Preacher was twenty years younger, he had been relieved when Eve grabbed Ben. Ben had apologized to everyone for the incident. As he walked away, Preacher spat blood at him, but Ben kept walking.

"Arthur," Jake said, letting go of Preacher's shirt. "You aren't worth wasting my time." With that, he got back in his truck and started the engine. He had driven only a few feet when he heard a thump, thump sound.

"Flat tire," he said to himself and hit the dash with his fist. He got out, inspecting the damage. The back tire on the passenger's side was completely flat. He looked at it closer. The cap had been removed from the stem, and a broken match was holding the valve core down, letting the air escape.

"Preacher!" he yelled, and turned to see Preacher's truck disappear around the corner.

Chapter 19

Ben Patton strained to lift the limb of the mulberry tree off the barbed wire fence. The rains of the past two days had left the pasture wet and slick, which made it difficult for him to get any leverage. The high winds had blown limbs down at several points, and Ben had spent the entire morning sawing limbs and mending fences. The stormy weather had abated for the time being, and the fences had to be repaired before the cattle got into fields that had been plowed for spring planting.

Ben was particular about his fences. He insisted on locust posts, exactly eight feet apart and set in the ground two and a half feet deep. All his fences had five strands of number one barbed wire, even though most people only used four strands.

After several tries, he was able to move the limb enough to get a chain around it and pull it off with the tractor without pulling the rest of the fence down. He thought of the torn old tree. It had been there when he first bought the Patton place some forty years ago. The boys had killed their first squirrel in that tree. In fact, they killed squirrels there every spring. The tree still looked healthy and strong, but he knew it couldn't live all twisted and torn. It wouldn't be long before insects and disease began the decaying process. *I guess old age makes us all not quite as strong as we once were,* he thought.

Ben didn't look old, at least not as old as he was. His stride was strong and purposeful. He walked across the uneven fields like a man many years younger. He still had coal black hair and broad muscular shoulders. Most people his age would not be working as he did, but Ben liked to keep busy. He had a lot of nervous energy and couldn't sit still.

To him, work was just a habit, like sleep. He worked long hours every day, including Saturday. When he took a day off, it was to go fishing with Jake or some of his retired friends. Ben had no thoughts of retirement himself. One good thing about farming was that he could always find spare time to do the things he enjoyed.

That was the thing he missed most when he worked in a factory in the North. When he was farming, he could take time off to see his children play ball or relax with his family. When you worked for someone else, you had to adhere to their schedule.

Ben associated hard work with being healthy. He was rarely sick and was stronger than men many years younger. He hadn't been to a doctor in years and hoped to keep it that way.

His toughness almost equaled his strength. When he went to the dentist for a filling, he never used a painkiller. He didn't like the way it made him feel. He preferred to endure the pain instead of the medication.

His strength and hardiness made it difficult for him to tolerate those weaker and less energetic than he was. He was a hard man, not given to much conversation, except around close friends. He was unwilling, or unable, to tolerate poor judgment and mistakes other people made. Even his closest relatives often felt the harshness of his convictions. He disowned his youngest sister, Myra, for marrying an alcoholic. It wasn't so much that she married him, but that she stayed married to him after years of abuse and neglect.

He was never late and didn't mind getting his hands dirty with a little hard work. He had plenty of money to hire people to help him on the farm, but he seldom did. He wasn't too stingy to hire help, but he didn't think there was anything he couldn't do, and he didn't think anyone else could do it as well.

The Patton place was located on the highest hill in Boone Valley, less than a mile from the original Patton place. From "the hill," as locals called it, one had an exquisite view to the north and east of the majestic mountains. The road to the Patton place was lined with dogwood trees. In the spring, they were a spectacular sight, their pink and white blossoms adding a dash of color to the green fields.

"What are you doing?" Jake asked.

Ben looked up. "What are you doing sneaking up on a fellow like that?"

"I have you to thank for that bit of talent," Jake said. "Remember all those times you made me practice walking through the woods without making noise?"

Ben laughed. "I had to do something to make you quieter. When we first started hunting, you made as much noise as a wounded buffalo tromping. An animal could have heard you a mile away."

"Well, your teaching stuck," Jake said. "I am always sneaking up on people without trying to. Let me give you a hand with that."

Jake and Ben strained to move a large fallen limb. After several attempts, they got it off the fence. "If there are any more that big, we will have to saw them first," Ben said, bending over to catch his breath.

"What's the matter?" Jake asked. "You're not that old, are you?"

"Pretty old," Ben said. "It won't be long until this is yours."

"You'll live to be a hundred," Jake said.

"I don't think so," Ben said, shaking his head. "There's something I have wanted to talk to you about for a long time."

"There's not anything wrong with you, is there?" Jake asked.

"No, nothing like that. I have been talking to Grady Layne. He has a position open for the right person in his insurance business. He told me the job was yours if you were interested."

"Dad, I don't know anything about insurance."

"You're smart; you could learn."

"I don't know," Jake said.

"Grady will be retiring in a few years. When he does, the business would be yours."

"Dad, I'm comfortable doing what I'm doing," Jake protested.

"You don't get much accomplished by being comfortable," Ben said.

"I am doing what I have always wanted to do," Jake said. "I have already had one book published, and it is still doing well."

"Just how much money are you going to make from that?" Ben asked.

"Enough to do me until I get my next book finished," Jake said.

"And just when will that be?" Ben asked. "You've been working on it for two years, and you told me yourself that you have just started."

"I'll finish," Jake said.

"Yeah, but there's no guarantee that it will be as successful as the first one you wrote," Ben said. "That stuff is a crapshoot."

"You always told me that nothing in life was guaranteed," Jake shot back.

"Nothing is," Ben said, "but there are some things you can count on more than others."

"You farm because you enjoy it," Jake said. "Well, writing is what I enjoy."

"I understand, son, but I was fortunate enough to be able to make a good living doing what I enjoy," Ben said.

"And I'll be able to make a living doing what I enjoy, too," Jake shouted.

"Don't raise your voice to me," Ben said. "All I have ever wanted was what was best for you. You could still write. Lots of people write on the side."

"If I take another job, I'll never get any writing done, and you know it," Jake shot back.

"Your mother and I worry about you. We know you will want to settle down and get married, and we think you need something steadier before you get involved with someone," Ben said.

Jake picked up a large limb and threw it on the brush pile before responding, "Five years ago, all you wanted me to do was to follow my dreams. Now, I need to stop dreaming and join the real world."

"Five years ago, you were just eighteen. You needed to go to college and get an education. You certainly didn't need to get married to that girl right out of high school."

"That girl?" Jake said, his voice growing louder. "Her name is Shelby."

"I know her name," Ben said, trying to explain, "but you were both too young and—"

"I loved her, Dad," Jake said.

"Son, you were eighteen. You didn't know what love was."

"Well, I'm twenty-three, and I still love her."

"Your mother and I only want what's best for you."

"I know you do, Dad, but how do you know what's best?"

"If you don't want to get into the insurance business," Ben said, "how about farming with me? There is plenty for both of us to do. I need help around this place."

"Dad, I love this farm almost as much as you do. Right now, farming isn't what I want to do with my life. Maybe in a few years it will be, but I want to write."

Ben shook his head. There were things about Jake he would never understand. When Ben was young, a chance for a steady job was all he could hope for in life. He worked hard, often at two jobs, to get the money to buy this farm and better himself. That's what he wanted for Jake.

"You could buy more land. The Patton place could be a gold mine. The barns could be painted, even a bigger one built. You could get back in the walking horse business. Jake, you could do so much with it," Ben said.

"Dad," Jake said, "that was your dream, not mine. You have done everything and more to fulfill your dream. The name Ben Patton is known everywhere in the state. You've accomplished what you set out to do. I just want to realize my own dream."

"I'm going to pull this one out of the field," Ben said, pointing to a large cedar tree lying in the pasture.

Jake chained the tree to the tractor. "Do you need me to unhook you?" he asked.

"No," Ben replied. "I'm finished here. Go check on your mother."

With that, he started the tractor and headed across the field. Jake watched him until he was out of sight and then walked toward the house.

Eve saw Jake out of her kitchen window. She could tell by the way he walked that something was wrong. Jake had never been one to hide his feelings. She had seen that same look many times before, head down, slow, almost shuffling stride, arms hanging loosely by his side.

She remembered a high school baseball game in which Jake made the final out of the game with the bases loaded and the tying run on third base. He had walked off the field with that same dejected look. Other players tried to console him, but he never looked up.

"Hey, stranger," Eve said, opening the storm door and going outside to meet him. "You look like you just got beat up."

He looked up and smiled sheepishly. "That bad?" he asked.

"Yeah, pretty much," she said. "What's going on?"

"It just hasn't been my day. First, I had a little run in with Preacher this morning."

"What in the world did you and Arthur get into it about?"

"He was running down my book."

"Try to ignore him."

"It's not easy. I think he flattened my tire, as well."

She rubbed her hands soothingly across Jake's back. "I think he is jealous and resentful and—"

"And sorry," Jake interrupted.

"Jake, there is good in everybody; you just have to dig deep enough to find it."

"It would take a lot of digging to find any good in Preacher."

"Just keep looking, and you'll find it."

Jake sat down on the porch. "Mom," he said, after a long sigh, "Dad and I can't seem to go five minutes without arguing."

Eve suspected as much, but didn't let on. "What's the problem this time?"

"He is trying to live my life for me again," Jake said, trying to make her understand.

"What did he do?" she asked.

"He wants me to stop writing and take an insurance job or go to work with him on the farm."

"Jake, honey, I am sure your father doesn't want you to give up on your dream. It is just that he doesn't understand it. Ben and I both grew up when times were hard. All Ben knows is work. He had to work hard to get where he is today. He thinks hard work is the only way to success."

"Mom, I appreciate how hard he has worked and the things he has been able to accomplish. I know he wants what he thinks is best for me, but that's not what I want."

"Your dad grew up having to worry about basic needs and forget about 'wants.' It's hard for him to get past that way of thinking," Eve said.

"He got to live his dream," Jake said. "All I want is a chance to live mine."

"Dreams change," Eve said. "We don't always get to live out our dreams, and that's not always a bad thing."

"We got into it about Shelby, too," Jake said. "Dad doesn't have a romantic bone in his body."

"You don't know your Dad very well," Eve said. "Wait here; there is something I want to show you."

Jake moved to the swing. He couldn't imagine what she wanted him to see. After a few minutes, Eve came back with a glass of lemonade and a leather satchel. She sat down in the swing with Jake and handed him the glass. He took a long drink.

"That's great," he said. "Fresh squeezed, I presume?"

"Is there any other kind?" she asked.

"What's in the bag?" he asked, curious as to what it contained.

"What I have here is something precious to me. It is worth more to me than any diamond or worldly possession. I have saved them for many years. When I want to feel young again, I take them out and reread them."

Eve opened a bag and held it out for Jake to see. Inside were dozens of letters. "They are from Ben," she said. "Pick one and read it."

Jake reached in the bag. He felt like he had happened upon a buried treasure and was unsure how to hold it. The postmark on the envelope he selected read Cleveland, Ohio, Oct. 29, 1955. It was addressed to Miss Eve Parker. Jake opened the envelope and stared at the writing. The penmanship was neat and familiar.

> *My Dearest Darling,*
> *How is my dearest darling tonight? Fine, I hope. This letter leaves me feeling blue. I need you here with me tonight to give me some sugar and warm my bed. I can't wait until Christmas. It seems like a year since we were last together. I miss so much holding you in my arms. I am so lonesome and blue. The wind is blowing like March, and it is pretty cold, but not as cold as my bed is without you. I am sitting here wondering what my baby is doing this Friday night. I guess you are sitting by the fire if it is as cold there as it is here. If we don't tell your parents soon, what will we do when I come home? We may have to stay in the Moffit hotel. I hate for your parents to be mad at us, but we have to be together, don't we, sugar pie? We are old enough to be married, and they should understand. We should not have snuck off and got married, but I couldn't stand not being with you.*
> *Darling, if you were here you would have to make me stop kissing you, for I love you more each day. I have a pretty good apartment here and hope you can join me soon. Maybe one day we can have a pretty place of our own, high on a hill, with lots of shade trees all around. Maybe we could even have a boy—that is, if you want one. I have always dreamed of having a son.*
> *Darling, if you knew my heart tonight, you would never doubt how much I love you. I hope to get a long letter from you*

tomorrow, but doubt I will since I mailed yours Monday. We will talk about nursing school once we are together.

I love you, darling, and I have never cared about anyone else like I care for you. I knew all the time you was meant for me, and as long as I live, I am only yours. I wish I could see you now. I hope you are thinking of me. I love you now and forever.

All my love,
XXX Ben XXXX

Jake sat stunned for several seconds after finishing the letter. "I can't believe that is from Dad," he said. "What was going on? Were you married and living apart?"

"My mother didn't want me to get married. Your father and I had been courting for a long time. We decided we couldn't wait any longer. We went to the courthouse and got married. We didn't tell my parents for almost a year. Ben went back to Ohio, where he had a good job. He worked overtime and saved every penny he could until I was able to join him."

"I can't believe you lived apart that long," Jake said, trying to fathom all he was hearing.

"My mother was sick, and we didn't want to upset her. I was her baby, and she was dead set against me getting married. It wasn't anything against Ben, it was just that I was her baby," Eve said.

"Wow!" Jake said. "I had no idea."

"Not too many people did," Eve said. "We kept it pretty quiet. My sister Grace knew, and Ben's brother Rob, and that was about it."

"I am sure it must have been difficult," Jake said, "living that far apart."

"It was," Eve said. "We wrote each other twice a week. There are lots of letters in here." She turned the satchel to where he could see. "Of course, some of these were written before we were married, when Ben was away working other jobs."

"I still have trouble seeing my Dad writing things like "my dearest darling" and telling you how much he wanted some sugar."

"We were young at one point, just like you are. Don't ever forget that. Times change, but when you come right down to it, people are basically the same. They have the same wants, desires, and needs as people in any generation."

"Why were you and Dad so against Shelby?" Jake asked.

"We weren't against Shelby," Eve explained. "Ben and I had been in a similar situation. You were our baby. Ben and I just felt that you were both too young to make such a commitment. We wanted you to go to school and get an education."

"But I loved her, Mom," Jake said, his voice cracking.

"And I loved your Dad," Eve said, "and we waited until we had saved some money and were more stable before we got married."

"But I lost Shelby," Jake said. "I lost her."

"If it had been true love," Eve said, "she would have waited, like Ben waited on me."

"She didn't know why I broke up with her," Jake said. "I didn't know what to tell her. I was too hurt to even talk to her about it. I just told her I wanted to break up, and I wouldn't talk to her about it."

"Son, I am so sorry. Ben and I worried that we made a mistake by trying to make your decision for you. We just wanted what was best for you. If we are guilty of anything, it was wanting to make sure you didn't mess up your future," Eve said.

Jake sat with his head down for a long time. Eve sat in the swing, not sure what else to say, fearing anything said might make things worse.

Jake opened the letter and read it again, slowly, as if he was absorbing each word.

"What's this about nursing school?" he asked after a long pause.

"That was my dream," Eve said. "One that was never fulfilled."

"Why not?" Jake asked. "What happened?"

"First of all," Eve said, "Ben didn't want his wife to work outside the home. I know that is old-fashioned, but at that time, most women didn't work outside the home."

"Dad is pretty stuck in his ways," Jake said.

Eve nodded. "I may have had to forget that dream, but I have never regretted it. I have had a wonderful life with your dad. There is still no one I had rather spend time with, even after all these years."

"That's great, Mom," Jake said. "I bet not too many people can truthfully say that."

"Jake, your dad loves you more than anything in the world. I will never forget how happy he was when you were born. We had been trying to have another baby for ten years, but I could never get pregnant. We had all but given up, but then one day, I found out I was expecting."

"How old were you?" Jake asked, trying to calculate the years.

"I was thirty-eight," Eve said. "Pretty old to be having a child. Ben waited on me hand and foot when I was pregnant. He wouldn't let me do anything. You would have thought I was an invalid. He wouldn't even let me cook."

"That's hard for me to imagine," Jake said. "I can't see Dad in the kitchen cooking breakfast."

They both laughed. Jake reached over and hugged his mother. "Thanks for sharing this with me, Mom," he said. "It's really helped."

Chapter 20

Bobby Jack arrived back at Preacher's a few minutes before eight. Rain was coming down in sheets, but he couldn't sit in the truck until the weather let up. He dashed through the rain and bound into the house. Rusty, Martin, and Preacher were sitting around the kitchen table, smoking joints. "Take a hit of this," Preacher said. "Looks like you need it."

He took a couple tokes but still couldn't calm down. "What if Dennis don't show up?" he asked.

"We'll do it without him," Rusty said.

"What if he has told somebody?"

"Just calm down," Preacher reassured him. "He'll be here."

Bobby Jack walked to the window and peered into the darkness. "What if he don't show?" he said again.

"He'll be here," Preacher said, trying to reassure him. "Come on over here and sit down."

Bobby Jack went to the table and sat down. Preacher was talking about something, but Bobby Jack couldn't concentrate. "Did you hear that?" he said. "Somebody is out there."

"It's just the wind," Rusty said.

Bobby Jack got up and looked out the window again. "I'm sure I heard somebody out there," he said. He stared out the window for several minutes before returning to the table.

Preacher was telling a story about hunting. "Damn biggest coon I ever seen," he said, "Every dog I had was scared of it. It was about to—"

"I saw a light!" Bobby Jack said, jumping up again to look out the window.

Headlights broke through the deluge and flashed across the room. It was raining so hard he could barely make out the outline of the vehicle, but he was certain it was Dennis's battered truck.

After several minutes, the rain let up, and Dennis opened the door. Without speaking, he removed his camouflage coat and shook the rain from his curly hair. Like Preacher, he was wearing cowboy boots and a flannel shirt. A large chew of tobacco was in his jaw, and he carried a Styrofoam cup filled with a paper towel to spit the juice in.

"About time," Bobby Jack said.

Dennis looked at him sullenly, but didn't say anything.

"Sit down," Preacher said, and they gathered around the table. Preacher adroitly rolled a few more joints, on which the others eagerly toked. Smoke drifted toward the ceiling. Preacher reached in his pocket, got out a couple pills, popped them into his mouth, and swallowed without water.

"Is that all you got?" Bobby Jack asked.

Preacher reached under the table and got a small bag that had been taped underneath. "Damn, Preacher," Bobby Jack said, his eyes narrowing as he looked at the bag. "You've been holding out on us. This is more like it."

"If we do this right, there will be plenty for all of us," Preacher said. "After you tie them up, look everywhere for money. Look in shoes, drawers, jacket pockets—anywhere they might hide cash."

"Maybe they got jewelry, too," Bobby Jack added.

"Anything we can sell, we will take, but nothing hard to carry. We don't want any damn TVs or anything like that," Preacher continued. Preacher went over the details of their plan, seeming to enjoy the attention and status.

Martin sat on the bed, his back against the wall, the rickety springs creaking with his every movement. While the others huddled around Preacher's table as he went over the last minute details, Martin stared intently at his name tattooed on his forearm, flexing his muscles to make it move.

A wood stove provided heat in the wintertime, but on cool nights like tonight, Preacher burned a small kerosene heater. Dirty dishes were piled high in a rusty sink, and the olive linoleum that covered the entire house had rotted in places around the wall where the roof had leaked and water had stood.

The sound of the rain crashing down on the tin roof forced them to raise their voices and struggle to hear Preacher over the vibration. It appeared that the rain had set in for the night, and Dry Creek had already begun to rise. The moon wouldn't be shining, so they would have the veil of darkness.

Preacher took the bag and opened it carefully. It contained four or five chalk-colored particles.

"This stuff looks right," Rusty said.

"It should," Preacher said. "You can thank the cook over there," he said, pointing to Martin.

"That's all we got now," Martin said, getting up to join the others, "but in a few days, we will have plenty."

"Hold this," Martin said, handing Bobby Jack a large spoon. He lit a small propane burner and put one of the rocklike particles in the spoon. Bobby Jack held it for him.

"Let me add a little of this," he said, taking an eyedropper and dropping three drops of water. The water hit the crystals, and it turned into thick, syrupy liquid.

Martin produced a syringe. "I get the first lick," he said.

He pulled three units into the syringe and injected it into his arm with the skill of a doctor. Bobby Jack followed.

"What about you?" Preacher asked Dennis.

"I've been clean six months," he said, taking off his cap and rubbing his hands through his hair. Though it was cold, he was sweating profusely, helpless to resist the lure of the drug.

"You ought to try it, Preacher," Martin said. "It will make you fly."

"I've done all the flying I want to," Preacher said.

Martin was starting to feel the rush. He had cold chills all over his body. He felt his heart beating faster. It was getting hot. He took his coat off. *Maybe Bobby Jack was right. Maybe somebody was outside.* He went to the window and looked. He couldn't see anything in the rain.

"Maybe I will take a little hit," Dennis said. He put the remaining amount in the syringe and injected it.

They sat around for some time, enjoying the euphoria. After a long spell, Preacher stood up. "It's time to go, boys. I wish I was able to go with you."

"Take this," Preacher said, handing Bobby Jack a .22 caliber snub-nosed revolver. He took another like it and handed it to Martin.

"Where the hell did you get these?" Bobby Jack asked.

Preacher shrugged. "None of these have serial numbers on them. If you get in trouble, just throw it away."

He handed Dennis a .38 revolver. "Check to make sure you know how to use them," Preacher ordered. Each of them checked his weapon out carefully, switching it back and forth in their hand until they became accustomed to the feel. Boxes of shells were thrown on the table, and the three began loading their guns and stuffing extra shells in their pockets.

Rusty kept his hands in his pockets. "Ain't you got a gun?" Bobby Jack asked.

Rusty nodded. "Mine is right here in my pocket." The others looked at Rusty for a minute and then went on with their business.

"Here are ski masks for each of you," Preacher continued. "Just kick the door in, tie them up, get what you can, and get the hell out. Bring whatever you get back here, and I've got a guy that will buy it."

Everyone nodded in agreement. "Damn, boys," Preacher said. "I wish I could go with you, but you know how my back is. I'd only slow you down."

"We'll be fine," Rusty said.

Dennis wasn't so sure, but he didn't say anything. Martin was just a kid. Bobby Jack was geeking big time, and Rusty was crazy. Dennis distrusted people, and he had the most doubts about Rusty. *What the hell was he doing here?*

"Bring the stuff here as soon as you can," Preacher said again. "We'll get rid of it fast, and no one will be the wiser."

They walked out on the porch. The rain was still beating down on the tin roof, and Dry Creek had turned into a raging stream. Preacher shouted some final instructions, and three men dashed through the rain to the waiting truck provided by some friends on the mountain that owed Preacher a favor. Rusty lingered on the porch, talking to Preacher. Rain danced on the hood, each droplet coming to life for a brief instance before streaming down the side to become part of the ever-increasing river of water.

"Is he coming or not?" Bobby Jack asked. Rusty remained on the porch, nodding agreement at Preacher's final instructions. When the lights came on, he bounded off the porch and climbed into the cab of the truck.

Chapter 21

Eve was reading *An Hour before Daylight* by former president Jimmy Carter when Ben Patton finally came to bed. She and Ben had visited Plains, Georgia the summer before and spent three wonderful nights in the Historic Plains Inn. The Plains Inn had seven rooms, each decorated in the motif of a specific decade of the twentieth century. Ben and Eve were amazed that a town no bigger than Plains had produced the thirty-ninth president of the United States.

They visited the farm where President Carter was born and raised. It reminded Ben so much of the farm where he had grown up. The Carter farm had more modern conveniences, but the similarities were obvious.

They had also visited the school Mr. Carter attended. Seeing the old flattop desks and classrooms brought fond memories to Eve and Ben, but the highlight of the trip had been Sunday school at the Maranatha Baptist Church. President Carter had taught the class, which was attended by about three hundred people, mostly visitors there to see the former president.

After church, Secret Service agents herded visitors in lines to have their picture made with the president and his wife, Rosalynn. Mr. Carter had asked them where they were from, and Ben had said proudly that he was from Tennessee. After a quick snapshot, they were escorted out, and another group took their place. It had taken only a few seconds, but it had made lasting memories.

"I see you are still reading about Mr. Carter," Ben said. "How many books of his have you read now?"

"This is the third one," Eve said. "I'm too busy to read much."

"It's pretty amazing," Ben said. "When he was president, nobody liked him, and now that he is out of office, everyone loves him."

"Well, he has done a lot of humanitarian things. He's always going somewhere and doing something to help people."

"I guess you are right," Ben said, getting into bed. "He is pretty busy for an old codger."

Eve laughed and closed her book. "Let's see," she said. "How old are you?"

Ben leaned over and kissed her gently. "I'm not too old."

"Oh, Ben! I love you so much. You know you will always be my handsome young prince."

They hugged each other for a long time, not wanting to let go of the feeling of youth and desire.

"What did Jake have to say?" Ben asked, breaking a long silence.

"He told me you two had a little argument," Eve confessed, laying her head on Ben's chest.

"We can't seem to talk without him thinking I am trying to control his life."

"Dear, I once heard someone say that raising a child is like a relay race; for a very short time, the two of you are running together, but before long you have to hand the baton off and let him run his leg of the race on his own."

"I didn't know you were a philosopher, too. Now I know why I married you."

"Oh, Ben, you are such a tease," Eve said, giving him a big hug. "Do you remember when we were courting? Do you remember how we couldn't wait to be together?"

"How could I forget?" Ben said. "The weeks seemed like months when we were apart."

"Remember how we felt when my mother threatened to disown me if we got married?"

"I remember," Ben said. "I didn't think I would ever be able to forgive her."

"Well, Jake feels like we prevented him from being with Shelby," Eve said.

"We were only trying to do what we thought was best for him."

"Just like my mother thought she was doing what was best by keeping us apart."

"That was different."

"How was it different?" Eve asked.

"Your mother was so unreasonable."

"And Jake thinks we were unreasonable."

"We never meant it that way."

"I know, honey," Eve said, "but the results were the same. What if my mother had prevented us from getting married?"

"We'd have run away," Ben said, getting flustered.

"Jake respected us enough not to do that," Eve said, "and he lost the girl he loved because of it."

"This is different."

"Ben," Eve said, "we made his decision for him about Shelby, and it turned out wrong. We can't control his decision about his career, too."

Ben stared at the floor for a long time. "I guess you are right," Ben said dejectedly. "I'll talk to Jake tomorrow and tell him to do what he wants to do with his life. He's an adult, and he is capable of making his own decisions."

"That's why I love you so much," Eve said. "You always know when to do the right thing." They hugged like young lovers before drifting off to sleep.

At 12:45 AM, Eve awoke with a bad case of indigestion. She had been bothered by acid reflux over the years, but lately it was getting worse. She slipped out of bed and went downstairs to get some medicine.

On the way back upstairs, she heard a noise. She stopped and listened, but didn't hear anything. She started toward the door to see what was making the racket.

"Rowdy, if you are in the garbage can again, I will—"

The door burst open, and four men in ski masks rushed into the room. Eve tried to run, but was grabbed by one of the men before she got to the stairs. "Ben!" she screamed. One of the men wrapped his hand across her mouth.

Ben was awakened by the scream. He grabbed his gun and ran down the stairs. When he reached the landing, he saw Eve being held by four masked men.

"What do you want?" Ben asked, his voice a little unsure.

"Put down your gun or she's dead," Rusty said, putting his pistol to Eve's head.

Ben placed the pistol on the floor without hesitating.

The men herded Ben and Eve together into the kitchen where one could watch them while the others ransacked the house.

"What are you guys looking for?" Ben asked, trying to get their guard to talk to them. The guard just shook his head. Ben watched how he held the gun awkwardly, hoping for an opportunity to escape. While the gunman looked to see what the others were doing, Ben edged Eve closer to the door. She held his arm tightly. Their eyes met, and she understood what he was trying to do.

Ben reached his arm behind his back and began to turn the doorknob. It made a small click. The guard was too busy to notice. Ben eased the door open an inch at a time. Just a little farther… Creak! The door made a loud noise. The guard looked at Ben and Eve. "What are you up to?" he asked.

"We are just keeping each other warm," Ben said, hugging Eve.

"What was that sound?" the guard asked. He walked over to where Ben and Eve were standing.

Though he was nearly a foot taller than Ben, the older man squared his shoulders and looked him straight in the eye. "Must have been thunder."

"Didn't sound like no thunder I ever heard."

"Why don't you take off that mask so you can hear better," Ben said.

"You're really a funny old man. You must think I am pretty stupid."

"No, son," Ben said. "I think you need help."

"Looks to me like you're the one that needs help."

The guard walked back to the living room. "Ya'll hurry up!" he shouted.

The instant he turned his head, Ben opened the door and pushed Eve through it into his study. The door didn't have a lock. Ben looked around and found a chair to use as a scotch. The guard yelled for the others, and they began beating at the door.

"You might as well come on out," one of them yelled.

Ben went to the window. He saw one of them coming around the house toward the window. There was no use trying to go that way. He closed the curtain and went to the closet. He didn't keep guns in the closet. He always put them back in the safe. This was one time he wished he wasn't so steadfast about being organized. He searched vainly for a weapon.

"Ben!" Eve screamed as the top part of the door burst into splinters.

Ben pushed Eve to the back of the room. "Get down and stay down," he said.

He grabbed a chair and waited. The door came crashing down. The burly robber was thrown off balance when the door gave way, and he fell to his knees. Ben swung with all his might and brought the chair crashing down on the fallen man's back. He collapsed to the floor. Ben grabbed the second robber as he came through the door and threw him against the wall. He was about to throw a punch when he was tackled from behind.

"Get up, old man," the tall one said, pointing a pistol at Ben's forehead.

Ben staggered to his feet, holding the shoulder that had been driven into the hardwood floor. "Are you all right?" Eve asked.

Ben nodded. "If I'd just had a gun in the closet—"

Eve squeezed his arm gently. His jaw jutted out the way it always did when he was angry. Eve wasn't sure if Ben was more upset with their predicament or the fact that he had tried and failed to escape. Failure was something Ben Patton did not accept easily.

One of the robbers grabbed Ben and pushed him down in a chair. "We've searched the house. Where the hell do you keep your money?"

"I don't keep much money at the house," Ben said.

The leader stuck his gun in Ben's face. "You better find some."

"My billfold is upstairs," Ben said.

He pushed Ben toward the stairs. Two others followed, and one kept Eve downstairs. Once upstairs, Ben gave them his billfold. They opened it and took out seventy-two dollars.

"Is that all you got?" one of the men said.

"There're a few coins in the closet," Ben said.

One of them went to the closet and pulled out several books of coins. They placed them in a pillowcase along with the jewelry and other things they had found in the house.

"Go downstairs," the leader ordered the other two. They complied without speaking,

Once they were gone, Ben began to worry. He knew what was coming and tried to talk to the robber. "You got everything we have," he said. "Just go and let me and my wife alone."

"Can't do it, Mr. Patton," he said, dragging out the mister. "My orders are to tell you who sent me before I kill you."

"What are you talking about?" Ben asked, startled.

"Preacher sent me. I guess I owe him one."

"Why would Arthur want—"

Rusty fired before he could finish the sentence. Ben spun and fell to the floor, blood staining the front of his shirt. Rusty nudged Ben's body with his shoe. Satisfied that he was dead, he walked back down the stairs.

"Oh, God! Oh, dear God!" Eve screamed when she heard the shot. "Ben!"

Bobby Jack had to grab her around the waist with both hands to keep her from running toward the stairs. When she saw

Rusty come down the stairs alone, she began to sob uncontrollably.

"Where are you hiding the money?" Rusty asked again.

She continued to cry, unable to answer. Rusty slapped her with the back of his hand. "Answer me, damn it!" he yelled. He slapped her again, and she fell to the floor.

"Shoot her," he said to the others.

No one made a move. They fidgeted, looking at each other.

Eve got up and ran for the stairs. The three men looked at her, but none aimed their guns. Rusty fired one time, hitting Eve in the side, knocking her to the floor, breaking a small table.

Upstairs, Ben was badly wounded, but alive. He found his sixteen-gauge Winchester pump shotgun in a wall panel where he hid it. He could barely move his left arm, but he loaded the gun and started for the stairs.

He heard the shot before he got halfway down the stairs. He saw Eve tumble across the floor. He bent down and opened fire. They ran for cover. He didn't have much protection where he was. He had to get off the stairs. Only one of the robbers was returning fire. He fired in rapid succession to keep them from shooting at him. One of the robbers made a break for it, but Ben shot him and sent him reeling to the floor. He appeared to still be alive, but he wouldn't be shooting anyone else.

Ben ducked behind a chest at the bottom of the stairs. He had to get to Eve. He saw her on the floor. "Eve!" he cried.

Her eyes turned toward him. She tried to speak, but no sound came out.

"I'm coming for you, babe," Ben yelled before firing another quick shot.

Eve reached her hand toward Ben. He fired again and ran to her side. He tried to pull her behind the desk, but he was weak from loss of blood, and she was unable to help him. Another shot ripped into his back. He tried to fire at his assailants as he sank to his knees.

"I love you, honey," he said, and slumped down on top of her.

155

Chapter 22

The noise woke Gary from his sleep. He looked at the clock. It was 1:30 AM. The sound had been almost too faint to hear, but Gary Simms was a light sleeper. Had he gone to bed instead of falling asleep on the couch, he would never have heard the muffled gunshots.

Two years in the jungles of Vietnam made one take notice of the sound of gunfire. Though it had been more than twenty years, he still was in the habit of processing information every time he heard a gunshot. Was it a rifle? No, sounded like a 9mm and a shotgun. There was a shot from the 9mm and a long pause. Two shots from the 9mm followed almost immediately by two shotgun blasts. Three more shots from the 9mm fired rapidly, then several shotgun blasts, followed by the sound of the 9mm. There was a long silence and one final blast from the 9mm.

It came from the Patton place. Uncle Ben wouldn't be shooting at anything this late. He had to find out what was going on. He picked up his pistol and threw on a long raincoat.

It was probably nothing, he kept telling himself. Still, he didn't want to take chances. He jumped in his truck and started down the lane. There was a light on at Jake's house, and he decided to stop.

Jake answered the door after the first knock.

"What are you doing out this time of the night?" he said.

Gary Simms ducked instinctively as he came through the door.

"I heard shots up toward Uncle Ben's house," Gary said, "Thought I had better come and let you know."

"That's strange at this time of the night," Jake said.

"You better call and check," Gary continued.

Jake picked up the phone and dialed his parent's number. "Busy. It's late for the phone to be busy," Jake said. He hung up the phone. "I guess we better go see what is going on."

Jake threw on a coat, and the two men hopped into Gary's truck. Jake rode along in silence. He could tell how serious Gary thought it was, and he began to worry.

"You expecting trouble?" he asked, noticing Gary's pistol holstered to his belt.

"Just cautious," Gary said. The rain continued to pour, and the bursts of lightening came so close together that the sky was lit constantly.

They turned into the lane that ran to the Patton place and were startled by the headlights of a truck at the top of the hill. Gary stopped and tried to stare through the blanket of rain. After several seconds, the truck began moving toward them.

"Get down!" Gary yelled. He slid the truck sideways to block the road. The words were barely out of his mouth when bullets shattered their windshield. Gary bolted out the door, and in one motion fired five shots into the other truck as it tried to back up the hill. The pickup careened into the ditch and slammed into a pine tree.

Lightning flashed, and Jake saw the occupants of the truck scramble out and run into a plowed field, leaving the smoking, hissing truck for the safety of the night. Jake climbed out of the truck. Gary replaced his clip and came around to check on Jake.

"You okay?"

"Yeah, how many are there?"

"Four got out of the truck and ran into the woods. I don't think there is anyone left inside the vehicle."

"What were they doing?" Jake asked, still dazed.

"I don't know," Gary said, getting a rifle out of his truck and giving it to Jake, "but we better find out."

"How did you know they were going to shoot at us like that?" Jake asked as he checked the weapon to make sure the safety was off.

"Just had a feeling, that's all."

Jake let it drop, but he couldn't help but think there was more to it than that. Gary had been a ranger in Vietnam. He had received a chest full of medals, as well as two bullet holes. At a small hamlet near Binh Gia, his company had been ambushed. Two guerrilla regiments wiped out his entire battalion. Nearly four hundred officers and men were killed, wounded, or captured.

Though wounded badly in the shoulder, Gary crawled through the jungle for five days, evading Vietnamese patrols, to get back to his own lines. He had never had much to say about his two tours of duty, just that he was doing his duty.

"Let's go check it out," Gary said.

They inched up the hill toward the smoldering dragon.

Gary motioned for Jake to move to the other side of the truck and cover him. Jake nodded that he understood. Though it was a cool, rainy night, he was sweating profusely. Jake edged up the ditch, moving quietly on his toes, as his father had taught him to do when they were hunting. His fingers nervously caressed the trigger. The closer he got to the truck, the harder his heart pounded. The gun felt heavy in his hands. Gary was in position and nodded to let him know he was ready. Jake aimed his rifle at what was left of the windshield and watched for any sign of movement. Everything was quiet; the only sound was the hissing of steam escaping from the radiator. Time stood still.

Gary yanked open the truck door, but it was empty.

"I must have hit one of them pretty bad," Gary said, pointing to the blood in the seat. "I was just aiming for the front of the truck." He looked for bullet holes in the seat, but couldn't find any.

It was beginning to rain harder. Gary walked over to Jake and pulled him close to keep from having to shout over the crashing rain. "We got to go check on your folks," he said. "Just try to relax; you're about to squeeze that gun in two."

Jake looked at his hands, a little embarrassed. "Okay," he said, and nodded for Gary to go ahead. They proceeded up the hill, careful to avoid walking into a trap. Gary lay down on the bank and scanned the area. The men in the truck had run back toward the house. They could be anywhere. Jake knelt behind Gary, fighting back his impulse to run to the house and check on his parents.

"There's a light on in the bedroom," Gary said.

Jake could see the lights on inside the house, but there was no sign of movement. Inch by inch, they made their way to the edge of the porch.

"Keep me covered," Gary said as he slid onto the porch. Jake marveled that a man his size could move so effortlessly and quietly. Gary tried the front door, only to find it locked. Gary motioned Jake toward the back of the house. They slipped past the rose bushes and crawled to where they could see the back door, Gary leading, Jake silently following.

"The door has been kicked in," Gary said, pointing to the white wooden door that led into the back of the house. Even through the rain and darkness, Jake could see that a muddy boot print stained the white door.

Chapter 23

Gary opened the door with the barrel of his gun and peered inside. Jake could see the usual assortment of flowers his mother kept there. On the wall to the left were shelves filled with vegetables his mother had canned. Ben's hat lay on the washing machine, along with a pair of dirty pants.

It was quiet, the rain had let up, and there was no sound. All Jake heard was the sound of his own heart beating. He wondered if Gary could hear it.

The door leading to the kitchen was slightly ajar. Jake wanted to rush in, but followed Gary's lead. They eased into the kitchen. Everything looked normal. A caramel cake sat half-eaten in a cake plate on the table. The dishes were stacked on a dishcloth, drying.

Gary became bolder. He no longer crouched, but stood up and moved to the entrance to the living room. The light from a downstairs room shone into the rest of the house. Gary pushed himself against the wall and raised his pistol. Jake readied his rifle. Gary spun low, pistol in front, and held his position, scanning the room. He cursed under his breath.

"It's bad!" he whispered. Jake pushed him aside and went in. Inside the house he had grown up in, Jake was bewildered. Furniture was turned over and clothes thrown all over the house. Only his trophies remained neatly in place on the mantle.

He looked around the room and became aware of something else. On the wall, by his father's recliner, there were dark stains. Slowly, he came to realize blood was splattered on the wall of the great room. Jake's eyes fixed on the blood. He moved closer; his heart pounded against his chest, his stomach in his mouth. There, lying in a pool of blood was his father, a hideous wound on the side of his head.

In the darkness, he almost didn't see her, but underneath his father's right arm lay the body of his mother, a gaping wound in her chest.

"Oh, God! Oh, God! Oh, Daddy! Mama!" he screamed. Tears streamed down his face. He fell to his knees and cradled his father in his lap. He rubbed his mother's hair. Her body was still warm.

"Why? Why?" he sobbed.

Gary examined Eve and Ben closer. After feeling for a pulse, he sadly shook his head. Eve had a single wound, but Ben had been shot three times, once in the shoulder, once in the stomach, and then in the head.

"Looks like he may have crawled over here trying to protect her," Gary said, pointing to the bloodstains on the hardwood floor that started across the room. Jake sobbed on his shoulder, unable to speak.

"Call the police. I'll track those bastards down," Gary said, tears streaming down his face.

For a moment, there was silence. "No, I've got to go myself," Jake sighed. He hugged his parents once more. He stood and immediately became sick. He ran from the room and vomited in the sink. It felt as if his insides were coming out. All feelings and desires were spilled in the spew that came from his soul and replaced with the thirst for revenge. After heaving until there was nothing left inside, he walked back to where Gary stood.

"Get Todd and Larry and go down toward Goodman's Mill and make sure they don't cross the highway at Grassy Ridge. I am going to go get Rowdy and track them," Jake ordered, drying his tears.

"I'm going with you," Gary protested.

"Somebody has got to keep them from getting to the road."

"Let me go after them," Gary said. "You can keep them from crossing the highway."

Jake shook his head.

"Damn!" Gary shouted. "Those are real guns they got. I know what I'm doing. It's my place to go."

"But it's my parents they butchered," Jake said.

Jake walked to the study, opened a wall panel, and picked up a flashlight and his father's twenty-two-caliber rifle. A Winchester pump, it was the first gun he had ever shot.

"Those guys have some heavy artillery. You better take more than that," Gary said, offering Jake his pistol.

"This will do fine," Jake said.

"I'll call the cops when I get to Todd's," Gary said. "Why don't you let me go?"

"No, I got to do it," Jake said, putting his hand on Gary's shoulder.

"At least let me go with you."

"I need you to keep them from crossing the main highway. They are headed toward the river, and it's flooded. They can't cross it. If they can't get across the highway, there is nowhere for them to go."

"Watch yourself," Gary said. "Don't get impatient. Let them make the mistakes. I'll meet you at the old mill."

The sound of rain could once again be heard on the tin roof. Jake left the house and ran to the barn to get Rowdy, half German shepherd, and half Doberman. Ben had named the dog for Clint Eastwood's character on the TV show *Rawhide*. The dog was locked up at night, and Jake couldn't help but think that his parents might still be alive if the dog had been loose. He had made this trip from the house to the barn a million times, but at this moment, it was the most difficult journey he had ever made.

The barn had sheds on both sides. The roof was steep and the loft filled with hay. The tin roof went up in three stages, all but the first too steep to climb. His father had insisted on painting it red, like the barns in New England, though few barns in the South were painted. Illuminated by lightning, the red paint looked like a mountain of blood and fire.

The rain mixed with tears, and the salty taste filled his mouth. He opened the door to the crib and let Rowdy out. The dog bounded out into the rain and shook himself. His rich black coat was soon drenched with rain, and he began to howl, as if he understood what had happened.

Chapter 24

Jake opened the gate and jogged down the lane to the field where they had last seen the four men. He wanted to stay out of the plowed field as long as possible. He ran through the peach orchard, past trees whose age-gnarled limbs were hidden beneath veils of pink blossoms, and crossed the fence at a sturdy locust corner post and plunged into the mud of the plowed field. He had trouble walking in the thick quagmire. Rowdy bounded over the fence and ran ahead.

Jake was certain the men he was after would be held up by the mud, and that by going down the lane and through the orchard, he would make up for lost time. The darkness was impenetrable, except for flashes of lightning that lit the entire countryside.

In the distance, truck lights raced down the road. He heard the sound of gunfire. It was Gary, making sure no one could cross the road toward Grassy Ridge. With all the shooting Gary was doing, it was unlikely they would go in that direction.

The other option was to try to cross the river. With all the rain the last couple of days, the river would be difficult to cross. The most likely place was Bell's Mill.

The flash of lightning cast a ghostly shadow on his lone figure as he sloshed through the muddy field. Rowdy trotted obediently at his side. Once he found their footprints in the field, their trail was easy to follow.

He wondered about his mother. Had she been afraid? Did she beg for her life? He knew she was afraid of guns, and he hoped—he had to stop thinking about it. He kept trying to piece together what had happened. Why were his parents downstairs that late at night? If his dad had heard someone breaking in, he would have gone downstairs by himself.

Maybe his father went down to investigate, and they shot him. His mother might have heard the shots and raced down to help him, and they shot her. That didn't explain why his father was on top, as if protecting his mother.

He stopped and almost threw up again. Tears filled his eyes, and he raised his face to the sky to wash them out with the rain. Why? Why? That was the thing that kept repeating itself in his mind. Why?

Chapter 25

The four men were having a difficult time in the sticky mire of the plowed field. They had started toward the road, but had taken a different route after seeing the spotlight and hearing the shots. They were back in the plowed field, and every step required great exertion.

"I've got to stop. Damn, I'm bleeding bad," Martin shouted above the pounding rain. A dark stain had soaked through his shirt and covered his jacket. The blood, diluted by the rain, dripped on the freshly plowed field. *Where had their plan gone wrong?* His thoughts were interrupted by the howl of what sounded like a wolf.

"What the hell was that?" Bobby Jack asked. "It don't sound like no dog I ever heard." Lightning flashed, and they saw the figure of a man on a hill less than a hundred yards away.

"Let's get the hell out of here!" Bobby Jack yelled.

Rusty grabbed the collar of his coat and stopped him in his tracks.

"It's only one man. Get your guns ready, and we'll blast the hell out of him the next time the lightning flashes."

Seconds seemed an eternity. The men waited, their weapons ready. A tremendous burst of light filled the sky, but the figure on the hill had disappeared. Without saying anything, the men tried to run through the ooze.

"I can't go on," Martin said, sinking to the ground in exhaustion. "My whole arm is numb. I think the bullet broke my collar bone."

"Damn it, you've got to move. The cops will be here before long, and somebody is following us. If you can't walk, we'll leave you," Rusty shouted.

"We ain't leaving nobody," Dennis said firmly. "Help me get him up."

Dennis and Bobby Jack began helping the wounded man, but the mud made walking almost impossible.

"We gotta stop," Bobby Jack yelled.

Rusty kept on walking. "Damn it, Rusty," Bobby Jack said. "We've got to rest."

"There's no way we are going to be able to get across the river with Martin hurt like he is," Rusty complained. "If we wait 'til daylight, the cops will be everywhere."

"Why in the hell did you kill them?" Dennis asked.

"If I hadn't killed that old man, he would have killed us all, you crazy fool," Rusty argued.

"God, it was awful. I never saw anyone killed before," Bobby Jack said. "How did we get ourselves into such a mess?"

"Shut up! All of you, just shut up," Rusty shouted. "You all had just as big a part in this as me."

"'Cept we didn't shoot nobody," Dennis said.

"You think any jury is gonna have mercy on you for that?" Rusty said. "Hell, no!"

"Over there're some woods," Bobby Jack said, pointing at a dark area a short distance away. Dennis and Bobby Jack helped Martin until they reached the edge of the woods. Out of breath, they clutched the trees like long lost lovers, inhaling deeply as they struggled for air.

At least it wasn't as muddy. The fresh odor of the damp woods, the resinous pines, and spicy sassafras brought a strange calm to the long night. They hadn't seen the man on the hill in some time, and thought they might have lost him in the dark.

Here they had protection, and the rain couldn't soak them to the bone as it had been doing in the open field.

"I'm freezing," Martin said, slumping to the ground once again.

Dennis went over and looked at his wound. "You've lost a lot of blood," he said. "We need to get that bleeding stopped."

Dennis looked at Bobby Jack. "Give me your tee shirt," he ordered.

"That damn rain is cold—" Bobby Jack started to protest, but after a stern look from Dennis he took his coat off so he could get to his shirt.

He handed the shirt to Dennis, who took out his knife and began shredding the shirt into strips.

"This is all we got to try to stop the bleeding," he said. "I'll do what I can, but this will probably hurt like hell."

Martin nodded. "It's killing me, anyway," he said.

Dennis pulled up the shirt and looked at the wound on his right shoulder. His collarbone was broken, and blood was flowing rapidly. He wouldn't live much longer if he didn't stop the bleeding. Dennis walked back out in the field and picked up a handful of mud.

"What the hell are you doing?" Bobby Jack asked.

We got to find something to pack in the wound to stop the bleeding," Dennis explained.

"But mud?" Bobby Jack asked doubtfully.

"You got a better idea?" Dennis asked. Bobby shook his head.

"Just hurry up!" Rusty said, irritated that it was taking so long.

"Go to Hell," Dennis said, staring at Rusty, who looked away.

"Do what you got to do," Martin said. "Just hurry, I'm dying."

"Hold him steady. I'll pack this in as much as I can," Dennis said. Bobby Jack held Martin securely. Dennis packed three hands full of mud into the wound then wrapped the torn strips of Bobby Jack's shirt around the injured area.

"That ought to stop the bleeding until we can get you somewhere to have that looked at," Dennis said.

"Thanks," Martin said, standing a little wobbly.

They helped him get his coat on and get to his feet. Dennis took out a cigarette and lit it. "This will warm you up," he said and handed it to Martin, who took a long drag.

Bobby Jack took the cigarette and began taking a puff. They heard a thud and then the sound of gunfire, but Bobby Jack would never hear anything again. A small hole appeared just above the bridge of his nose. A stain appeared on the flag he wore as a bandanna. His eyes stared ahead uncomprehendingly. His mouth was twisted with that same toothy grin. The world began to spin endlessly. He tried to speak, but no words came out. He wanted to move his arms and legs, but they were motionless. He fell face-first toward the earth, the sky exploded with a resounding crash, and then they heard a terrifying howl in the distance.

The three other men disappeared into the woods. They crashed through the thicket, briars and limbs tearing at their flesh. They staggered and slipped on the wet ground, tripped over stumps and logs, falling awkwardly to the ground as they blindly fought their way through the wooded maze. Their panic exhausted them before they escaped the dense forest.

The woods weren't large enough to offer much protection. The only hope for escape was through another plowed field on the other side of the woods. "Wait up!" Martin yelled, but companions kept running through the miry red clay.

Fatigued almost to the point of passing out, Martin looked around for a place to hide. He was too tired to run. The only protection he could find was a grown-up fencerow. He stumbled, fell, and lay curled up in a fetal position.

If he could get there and hide, no one would see him. He could barely find his way in the darkness. Whoever was after them would walk right past and not even notice.

If only he could get there. He staggered and fell in the mud. He had lost a lot of blood, and this clay mud stuck like glue. When he stood up, he felt light-headed, and everything spun and spiraled out of control. Was this what it felt like to die? No, he wasn't going to die. He was only nineteen years old. He couldn't die so young. The rest of them would probably be caught, but he would hide 'til he was feeling better, and no one would ever know he was a part of this mess.

It was supposed to be an easy job. Preacher had told them that the Patton's dog would be locked up and that the lock on the back door wasn't very solid. Rusty said they would kick the back door in and grab hold of the old couple before they had a chance to do anything. They would tie them up and rob the place. The plan had gone wrong from the start.

The old lady had been downstairs when they kicked the door in. What had she been doing up so late? Martin could still hear her scream when she saw what was happening.

Martin had seen the old man coming down the stairs with his gun in his hand, but he had been too scared to act. When the old man saw four men wearing ski masks in his house, he crouched to fire. Bobby Jack had saved them by grabbing the old woman when she tried to run for the stairs. When the old man saw they had her, he threw down his gun. Bobby Jack held a gun to the old man's head and tried to force him to tell them where he hid his money. Ben led them to where he kept his billfold, but swore that was all he had in the house.

After failing to find any more money, Rusty had shot him in the upstairs bedroom. They thought he was dead and began to threaten the old woman. She broke away and tried to run upstairs to check on her husband. Rusty shot her at the foot of the steps. After she fell, the old man came down the stairs with a shotgun.

His first blast sent them diving for cover. Rusty returned fire, but was driven back by a blast that shattered the kitchen door. Martin was convinced they would all be killed and tried to make a run for it. He had taken about three steps when a blast from the shotgun sent him sprawling across the table. He had tried to get up, but was forced to crawl back behind the stove.

The old woman was still alive and making gurgling sounds. Martin saw her trying to raise her head to see what was happening. She reached her hand toward the old man, as if pleading for help. Apparently unable to stand by and see her suffer, he had rushed to her side, firing several shots as he ran. He tried to pull her behind a desk, but she was unable to move on her own. After firing another shot, the old man attempted to pick her up, and Rusty shot him in the back. They fell together. The old man turned to fire one last shot. Rusty walked over and shot the old man again in the back of the head. He was going to shoot the old woman again, but Dennis told him she was dead already.

He hadn't fired a shot. Dennis hadn't, either. He didn't think Bobby Jack had. He just couldn't remember. *Who shot Bobby Jack? Where had the bullet come from?*

If only I could get to that fencerow. He began to crawl on the ground like a blind crab. Movement was slow. He dragged his body across the muddy terrain. Breath came in gasps, and blood bubbled from his lips. The rain and the mud mixed to form a mush, like quicksand, and he sank deeper with every move.

Lightning exploded across the sky. Out of the darkness in front of him was the silhouette of the man they had seen on the ridge earlier. He saw him a little clearer. He was wearing one of those long coats, like they wore in western movies. He was as large as a mountain. He scrabbled around, trying to find his gun. It wasn't in his pocket. Somehow, he had lost it in his attempt to free himself from the mud.

"Don't shoot! I surrender," Martin said, his voice cracking. "I'm hurt bad and need a doctor."

The figure never moved. "Who are you?" Martin asked, still searching for his gun. There was no reply. The silence was deafening. He heard a noise behind him. He turned and saw the ferocious teeth of a savage animal. The dog's black hair stood up on its back, and its mouth was open, showing slobber and fangs. A low growl came from deep in its throat.

A cry of horror came to Martin's throat but couldn't escape his mouth. He heard the word "Rowdy" and then felt a sharp pain as the animal's powerful jaws clamped onto his soft flesh.

Screams filled the air. Cries of horror and agony, too hellish for reality, filled the night. Dennis and Rusty heard the terrible screams, but there was nothing they could do. At last, the screams stopped.

"What was that?" Rusty asked when they stopped to catch their breath.

Dennis didn't answer.

"Did you hear those screams?" Rusty continued. Lightning flashed, and they heard another ghastly howl. They shivered from the cold of the rain and fear of the unknown. Their hands and feet were numb. The rain came down even harder. Walking was difficult in the gummy mud. If they were to escape, they had to get out of this mud.

"We got to get to the river," Dennis said. "It's shallow at Bell's Mill, and we should be able to cross the river there and make it back to Preacher's house."

The darkness was confusing. They walked for a good distance without talking. The rain and mud made traveling slow.

"How much farther do we have to go?" Rusty asked.

"Can't really tell in this mess," Dennis said. "Shouldn't be too much farther."

"You think we lost that man following us?" Rusty asked.

"It's awful dark," Dennis said. "I don't see how he could follow us."

"Damn," Dennis said as they neared the area where the old mill once stood.

They peered into the fog-shrouded darkness and were shocked by what they saw. The rain had caused the Elk River to overflow its banks. A lake of water stood between them and the place where the riverbank should have been.

"We have got to get across. Let's swim it," Rusty shouted over the crashing rain.

"Can't swim a lick," Dennis responded dejectedly. "You go ahead. I'll try to get down to the Gunn place and cross the bridge there. We'll meet at Preacher's."

173

Dennis watched Rusty disappear into the murky water then he slogged in the mud toward the shadowy wooded area near the water's edge. It was just a patch of trees on a knoll. Still, it was out of the plowed field and offered some protection from the rain. The water lapped against the side of the hill on the lower side. No one could get to him from that direction. All he had to do was watch the other direction and he would have a clear shot at whoever was following him. He didn't know if he could kill a man or not. He guessed he could if he had to.

Lightning flashed. *Tornado weather,* he thought to himself. The constant flash of lightning made it easier to see where he was going, but it was also easier for somebody to see him as he slogged, at what seemed like a snail's pace, across the open space. He crouched low, trying to be less visible.

This entire plan was doomed from the onset. They'd had nothing but bad luck, right from the beginning. Why had he gotten himself into this mess? Where was he going to go when he got out of here? Mexico? The law couldn't get him there, could it? Preacher always talked about Mexico. He'd need money to get to Mexico. Ah! The hell with Preacher, he thought, and the hell with Mexico; if he could make it to the mountains, he could hide out in the caves, and no one would ever find him. He knew the mountains surrounding the valley better than anyone did. Eric Rudolph had hid in the mountains for years with the FBI and everybody else on the lookout for him. He looked up. The patch of woods seemed as far away as before.

As he trudged through the mud, a thought came to him. His best chance of escape was to double back the way he had come. He might get by whoever was after him. Then he could easily cross the river at the bridge, walk around the ridge, and be at Blood Rock Cave before sunrise. No one would expect them to try to go that way, and in this darkness, no one would ever see him.

He was only a few yards from the woods when the storm hit with its full force. Enormous sheets of rain, driven by the stout west winds, crashed down on him. Gusts of wind nearly blew

Out of the Darkness

him off his feet. Trees in the woods bent low against the onslaught of nature.

Lightning hurled through the sky in jagged patterns, crashing to the ground with resonant vibrations. The fire bolts struck the earth and burst into fragments. The roar of the thunder was deafening.

Dennis tried to run, but it was impossible in the clinging mire. Beads of sweat spewed from every pore. God, he hated lightning. He winced and ducked every time it struck. He had always been afraid of it. He remembered when he was a little boy, staying with his grandmother near the Big Spring. Lying on her bed on stormy days, sinking deep into her feather mattress, she told him stories and warned him about the danger of lightning.

"Now don't fret your Granny," she'd always say, as she warned him about the two things she feared most—mad dogs and lightning. "Don't ever be out when it's storming, 'cause lightning don't care who it strikes. *Your uncle, Buddy Meeks, went out to shut a gate just before a storm hit to keep his milk cow from getting out, and while he was shutting it, lightning hit a tree and killed him dead on the spot. Some people say it's God's judgment. I don't know about that, but I do know you can't be too careful around lightning."*

He remembered when storms came. His grandmother would get in the bed with him and pull the quilts close. He always dreamed the mad dog she warned him about was chasing him, fangs showing and slobber coming from its mouth. He ran just ahead of it to his grandmother's house. When he got there, he was unable to get across the fence. He always woke just as the dog lunged at him. His eyes would bolt open, he would be sweating from the heavy covers, and the storm would be over.

He trudged on in what seemed to be an endless field of glue. His boots were too heavy with mud to lift. His breathing was labored, and thousands of tiny daggers pierced his side. At last, he reached the edge of the woods.

He climbed behind a hickory log and lay down. The struggle to walk had worn him out, but he could rest here and keep an eye out for whoever was after him. Every time the lightning lit up the sky, he could see all around the field. From this vantage point, no one would be able to get close to him.

The woods offered little protection from the downpour, and he shivered as the rain ran down the collar of his coat. He pulled his coat close and put his hands in his pockets to keep warm. The cold never had bothered him that much, but now he was chilled to the bone. Damn, it was cold.

A noise from behind surprised him. He turned too late. Rowdy's teeth ripped into his jaw, tearing his flesh. He tried to get his gun out of his jacket pocket, but the hammer of the .38 snub-nose kept hanging in the lining. Freeing his hands from his jacket, he began to swing excitedly at his attacker.

Blood gushed from his face. The animal ripped the flesh of his left hand to the bone. The two combatants tumbled down the hill and slammed into a tree. He gasped for air. The fall had knocked the breath out of him. In an instant, the animal was on top of him, tearing at his arm, and growling fiendishly. With all the strength he had left, he gave the dog a powerful heave and shoved it the rest of the way down the hill.

He barely had time to get his hand in his pocket before the beast was scrambling back up the hill. Unable to draw the gun, he raised the barrel and fired through his coat. Rowdy was in midair when the .38 slug crashed into his body, sending him tumbling to the sodden earth.

Dennis edged back against the tree and tried to stop the bleeding. It was useless, his blood flowed in a steady stream from his face, but it poured from his hand and arm in spurts. It reminded him of someone shooting a water pistol. He tried to apply pressure with his other hand, but the blood still gushed between his fingers. *Must be his artery*; he was bleeding to death. The blood mixed with the rain until the scene might have come from a horror picture. He took off his belt and wrapped it as tightly as he could around his arm. The bleeding slowed.

"I killed your damn dog; now you got to fight your own fight, you son-of-a-bitch. Here I am, come and get me," he shouted as he stood unsteadily. He squinted to see through the driving rain. When the lightning burst in the blackened sky, he saw the outline of a man near a small grove of pine trees. He began making his way toward the silhouette on the hill. When the next flash occurred only seconds later, the man had disappeared. Maybe he was seeing things? No, he was sure he had seen a man.

"Where the hell are you?" he shouted. Lightning flashed again, and there the man was, only ten yards away. Dennis raised his gun and fired. He ran, half-staggering, to where the man had been. Nothing! Not a sign.

He fell to his knees, the blood still pouring from his wounds. Again, the lightning flashed, and the form of a man loomed large in front of him. He raised his gun to fire, but was knocked backwards before he could pull the trigger. He reached his right hand down to his stomach. It was burning terribly. When he looked at his hand, it was covered with blood. He had been shot. He hadn't heard the sound of the gun firing. *Why hadn't he heard the sound? The rain? Or the thunder?*

Looking up, he saw the man that had been following him all the time. "Jake Patton—well, I'll be damned. I thought it was the devil himself following us. I never figured it was you."

Jake looked down at a man he had known all his life, but who now appeared a total stranger. Dennis's father and his father had been good friends when they were growing up. They had worked together for a logging company out on the mountain. Ben always did the hunting, and Henry did the cooking. Though Ben and Henry had grown apart, Ben always said no one could cook a mulligan like Henry. Jake and Dennis had been on the same little league baseball team.

"I'm real sorry about your ma and pa," Dennis said. "I sure never figured anything like this would happen. Rusty did it. He just went crazy. Preacher gave us the idea to rob your pa," Dennis rambled, still trying to stop the bleeding. "He said it wouldn't be hard to get in the back door and that the dog would be locked up. I never thought anyone would get killed. Are you going to kill me?" Dennis asked, already seeming to know the answer.

"I'm hurt bad, anyway; no need to kill me. Damn, I'm sure sorry all this happened. I ain't got a gun. I know you're a Christian man. I ain't much of a church-goer myself, but I do know Christians are supposed to be merciful." He waited for an answer, but none came.

Dennis looked down at the blood flowing from his hand and the wound in his stomach mixing with the rain and cascading to the ground. He tried to stand, but when he did, the treetops spun wildly.

He slumped back down on the wet ground and noticed his gun only a few feet away. If there was only some way he could get to it.

Jake hadn't said anything, and Dennis was certain his only chance was to try to get his gun. That wasn't much of a chance. His left arm was useless, and he was bleeding to death. Funny—he could hardly feel the bullet wound anymore. Wouldn't it be something to survive being gunshot and die from a dog bite? He had always heard how painful it was to be gut shot, but he didn't feel anything at all. Maybe that was it. Maybe he was dying, and it would happen without him knowing it. Panic overcame him. Life was slipping from his grasp.

He was overcome with fear and desperation. The gun—if only he could reach the gun. The sky lit up with a tremendous flash of lightning. The rumble of thunder broke the eerie silence, and then there was only the cadence of the rain as it beat down harder than before.

Dennis edged closer to the gun. Jake raised his rifle and aimed. His fingers tightened on the trigger.

"Don't do it," Gary Simms shouted.

Jake turned to see Gary only a few feet away. "He's one of the killers," Jake said. "He's one of them that killed Mama and Daddy."

"I didn't kill nobody," Dennis said.

"We'll let the police sort it out," Gary said. "He's about dead, anyway."

"No!" Jake shouted. "He deserves a bullet."

"Jake, look what you are doing," Gary said. "If you kill him like this, you are no better than they are. You know your mama wouldn't want you doing something like this."

"Just leave me alone!" Jake shouted.

Dennis saw his chance. He grabbed his pistol and fired. The bullet tore through Jake's coat. Gary and Jake ducked behind a clump of trees. With every ounce of strength he had, Dennis stood and stumbled down the hill. In the darkness, it was impossible for Jake and Gary to return fire.

Dennis stopped at an oak tree to catch his breath and get his bearings. If he could put some distance between them, it would be impossible to find him in the darkness.

He had to keep moving. He staggered down the hill. In the dark, he didn't see the rotting log at the bottom of the hill or the water beyond it. He tripped and fell headlong into the rushing water. He thrashed about violently, losing his gun in an effort to escape the vortex of water. He tried to stand, but the rush of water pulled him farther into the current. He was swept off his feet. His head went under, but he fought his way back to the surface. A dead tree branch momentarily prevented him from sinking, but his grip soon caused the limb to break, and he plunged to the bottom of the raging river. He struggled to hold his breath before succumbing, opening his mouth, and gulping in the rancid water.

"He won't get far," Gary said. "He's hurt bad."

"Help me find Rowdy," Jake said, looking around the darkness for his trusted friend.

He heard a low moan at the edge of some blackberry bushes. He rushed to the spot and knelt beside Rowdy, ignoring the briars that tore at his flesh and clothing. The first thing he noticed was the gaping hole in the animal's stomach. His black coat was matted with blood, and his insides had already found their way out of the opening and spilled on the ground. The dog was going to die, and Jake rubbed his blood-matted coat. Rowdy licked his hand.

Jake knew the humane thing to do was shoot Rowdy and put him out of his misery. He kept thinking about his mom and dad, and the dog was the last link he had to them. Even his mom had grown fond of the good-natured pet, though she often complained about the name. His dad had said he'd make a good watchdog, but he had kept him locked up at night because he didn't want the dog lying on the porch and getting everything dirty.

Jake didn't know if he could shoot him. Rowdy looked at him as if he was asking for help. He aimed his gun at the animal's head and looked into its helpless black eyes. Rowdy looked pitiful and frightened. Jake couldn't bring himself to kill his friend, even if it was for the best. He bent down, picked Rowdy up, carried him to a dry spot under a large hickory tree, and left him there.

"I still got to get Preacher," Jake said to Gary, who had been standing nearby, watching.

Gary nodded. "I'll go with you. I owe Preacher something."

"No. I need you to take care of Rowdy for me."

"Jake, there's nothing I can do for Rowdy."

"Just do what you got to do," Jake said, walking away.

After he had gone a few hundred yards, he heard a single gunshot. Gary had done what Jake was unable to do. Jake pulled his coat tight around him. The temperature had dropped drastically.

Chapter 26

Shelby paced back and forth considering what she should do. Rusty had left. He didn't tell her where he was going—only that he would be back later. She thought he might be going to meet one of his girlfriends, but she had seen him put his pistol in his coat pocket. He didn't know she was watching. She had been in the bathroom with the door partially closed, but she saw through the crack. He went to the dresser beside the bed and put it in the left pocket of his camouflage parka.

Why would he need his pistol? Maybe the person he was going to see was married, and he was worried about her husband catching them. She didn't care, just as long as he left her and Nicole alone.

The phone had been repaired earlier in the day, and she gave her parents a call. They worried about her. If her father knew half of what Rusty had done to her, he would have made her come home. They suspected Rusty was abusive—at least verbally, if not physically.

Shelby did everything possible to keep them from finding out. She hated to involve her parents in her problems. They had tried to convince her not to marry Rusty. Her mom had warned her before the wedding. "If you make your bed hard, you have to lie in it, anyway." Well, she certainly had made her bed hard. Her parents couldn't even imagine how hard.

Her father had heart trouble and didn't need any more stress. He'd had triple bypass surgery two years ago. Shelby was concerned about his health. She knew her mother shared her anxiety about him. She told Shelby every time he had the smallest ailment. The last thing he needed was something else to be anxious about.

Her father had missed several weeks of work due to his illness, and rumors were floating around that the plant where he worked was closing. He had worked there twenty-six years. There weren't many places where a middle-aged man in poor health could find a job. Shelby knew he was nervous about not being able to afford insurance for his family once he lost his job.

She picked up the phone and dialed the number. Her mother answered after the second ring.

"Hello, Mother," Shelby said.

"Hi, honey. Are you okay?"

"Yes, mom, I'm fine."

"Is Nicole all right?"

"She's feeling better. I think the medicine has helped."

"I worry about her. She seems so frail."

"Oh, Mother, she's fine. How's Dad?"

There was some hesitation. Shelby wondered if her mother had heard her. "He didn't feel well last night. I think he was hurting in his chest. We worked in the yard a little bit, but you know, these days Albert gets tired really easy."

"Make sure he doesn't try to do too much when he gets home from work."

"I guess you heard about the plant closing?"

"Hey, sugar pie," a gravely voice said.

"Hi, Dad. I didn't hear you pick up."

"I've been listening to you and Jean plan my funeral."

"Oh, Albert, we weren't doing any such thing. Shelby just asked how you were."

"Is Nicole better?"

"I was just telling Mom that the medicine Dr. Spangler gave her seems to be helping."

"I hear Spangler is pretty good, not like that quack I keep going to."

"Oh, Dad, I'm sure Dr. Wooten is fine."

"Sugar pie, if you need us for anything, just call."

"Thanks, Dad. Take care of yourself and make sure Mom takes good care of you."

"She's a slave driver."

"Oh, hush, Albert."

"Love you both."

"Love you," they said in unison.

Shelby hung up the phone. Her parents were always so jovial. She loved the way they teased each other. They had been that way all her life. She knew things hadn't always been easy for them, but they had stuck together, the two of them against the world. They might make fun of each other, but no one else had better try to do the same. She could never have that kind of relationship with Rusty.

She had to get away from Rusty. Somehow, there had to be a way out. She couldn't keep living like this. Even if he killed her, he wouldn't hurt Nicole. Being dead was better than living like this.

Shelby went to the sink and washed the dirty dishes she had used at dinnertime. She placed the dishes in the rack to dry. Before she finished, she began to cry. At first, she cried softly, but soon it came in incontrollable sobs. She tried to stop crying, catching her breath in long, choking gasps. She didn't want Nicole to hear her, but she felt so abandoned.

She dried her tears on a dishtowel. Her life had unraveled so fast. Things were only getting worse, and now Rusty had left the house with a gun. The uncertainty of the situation weighed heavily. She was suspicious. She knew Rusty sold pot and had had numerous affairs, but there was nothing she could do about it, nothing short of leaving him. She was scared to do that. She remembered the beating he had given her the first time she tried. Her arm still hurt where he had broken it. Still, that pain was not as bad as the pain she felt every day living in the same house with Rusty.

She got Nicole's medicine out of the cabinet and went to check on her. The little girl was lying in bed with her blanket pulled up under her chin.

"Hey, squirt. How are you?"

"I'm scared, Mommy."

Shelby sat down on the bed beside her. "What are you afraid of?"

Nicole pulled the covers back and sat up. "The thunder and lightning."

Shelby reached over and held her tight. "You're safe in here," she said, not wanting to let go.

They held each other for a long time. Lightning flashed and thunder rumbled, but neither seemed to notice.

"Who's that under the cover with you?"

"Sponge Bob."

"Is Sponge Bob asleep?"

"I think he is playing possum."

"Where did you hear that?"

"Mr. Jake said that today."

Shelby let go of Nicole. She straightened her pillow and buttoned the top button on her pajamas. "Mr. Jake said a lot of things."

"He's really nice," Nicole said.

"Yeah, I guess he is pretty nice," Shelby said, hating to agree with her.

"He's got brown eyes like me."

Shelby felt her face flush. "It's stuffy in here," she said, opening the window. The rain beat down steadily on the windowsill. "Enough about Mr. Jake. Let's talk about Sponge Bob."

"He's cool."

"He doesn't look too cool."

"He is."

Sponge Bob needs to get some sleep and so do you."

"Okay, he is pretty tired."

"Let's get him tucked in, so he can rest," Shelby said as she put him back under the blanket.

"We got to take our medicine."

"It's yucky," Nicole said, but opened her mouth and swallowed the spoonful without further complaint.

Out of the Darkness

"Sweet dreams."

"Don't forget our prayers, Mommy."

Shelby pulled the covers up tight under Nicole's chin. "Do you want to go first?"

"Why doesn't Daddy ever say prayers with us?"

Tears welled up in Shelby's eyes. She wanted to let out all the emotions that had been building up, but she knew Nicole wouldn't understand. "Daddy is busy," was the only answer she could muster.

They said their prayers, and Shelby said goodnight and went into the living room. She hated making excuses for Rusty. She was always doing that. Family gatherings, picnics, Christmas, and any other holiday required her to make some excuse why Rusty wouldn't be there, even if she were allowed to go. If not, she had to make up reasons why none of them would be there.

Rusty didn't like her family. They had always tried to be nice to him. When they were first married, her dad had invited Rusty to go hunting and fishing, but Rusty always turned him down. Her family was happy; Rusty didn't like it and couldn't understand it. They were always hugging and telling one another that they loved each other. Rusty had nothing to which to compare it. It made him uncomfortable. At first, she had gone to family outings without him, but more and more, he didn't want her to go, either. Not that he wanted to be with her, but he knew they were suspicious of him. He was afraid they might find out what he had done to her and force her to leave. Rusty had threatened to kill all of them if she ever left him. She was afraid to find out if he really meant it.

She put a compact disk in the player and sat down at the table to pay some bills. After writing the last check, she shook her head at the balance of $14.36. Rusty brought in money from time to time, but it was never anything she could count on. She had to watch every penny to make sure the electricity wasn't turned off. He had worked last week for Ralph Sanders, hanging sheet rock. She knew Ralph paid his employees well and paid them in cash. Rusty had given her two hundred dollars and kept the remainder to blow on who knew what. She wrote the check number on the paid bills and took them to her file folder in the closet.

In the back of the closet, covered with a garbage bag, was the black dress she had worn to the prom with Jake. She took it out and held it up to her. She wondered if it would still fit. She pulled off her shorts and tee shirt and slipped it on. It fit perfectly. She spun around and looked in the mirror. She felt like Cinderella at the ball.

The feelings and emotions came rushing back like a raging river. Pink Floyd's *Wish You Were Here* drifted through the air. She could almost feel Jake holding her as they danced.

She replayed every date in her mind. She'd felt like a princess in a fairy tale. She had never been treated so special.

She put her dress back in the closet and looked in on Nicole. She was sound asleep. Her forehead felt cool. The fever had subsided.

Shelby looked at the clock, picked up the phone, and dialed.

"Hello," the sleepy voice on the other end responded.

"Were you asleep?" Shelby asked.

"I'd just dozed off on the couch," Carrie said. "I get so tired now that I'm pregnant."

"Sorry I called so late."

"No, it's fine. Is everything okay?"

"Yeah, it's fine."

"Where's Rusty?"

"I'm not sure."

"What do you mean you're not sure?"

They had been friends for so long, and Shelby missed talking to Carrie. She was a good friend, and Shelby knew she could confide in her. "He left earlier this evening."

"Where'd he go?"

"I don't know," Shelby said, feeling foolish for even talking about it.

"Is he gone for good?"

"He said he would be back."

"I wish he was gone for good so you could get back to living."

Shelby didn't answer. She thought about trying to change the subject. "He took a gun," she finally said.

"What would he need a gun for?"

"I don't know," Shelby said, laying her head in her hands.

"You've got to get out of that mess."

"I don't see how I can."

"Come live with us. I'll shoot the bastard if he comes near my house."

"I can't do that to you. What would Buck think?"

"He's my husband, but you're my best friend. He will be all right with it."

"You're about to have a baby. I can't be a burden on you."

Carrie tried to protest, but Shelby changed the subject. They talked at length about everything since high school. After talking for over two hours, they hung up. Forty-five minutes later, Shelby's phone rang.

Chapter 27

Rusty waded into the water. It wasn't deep, but it was icy cold. The water was still, and he began to feel like he had a chance of making it to the other side.

He had gone less than a hundred yards when the swelling water began to move swiftly. It was already up to his chest, and the other side of the river was nowhere in sight. Suddenly, he stepped into emptiness. His head went under, and he gasped for air, thrashing about, trying to locate a foothold, but there was water churning all around him. He felt himself being sucked downstream by the current, but he was powerless to do anything about it.

He burst to the surface of the water, grabbed a breath of air, and plunged under again. *Why couldn't he stay afloat? Was this going to be the way he died?* He tried to swim, but was pushed under once again. Once more, he struggled to get to the surface. *What was dragging him to the bottom?* Across his shoulder, he still carried the money and other valuables they had stolen. The old man had many old coins, and they had put them in the bag. It was about to drag him into eternity. He struggled, but couldn't get the pack off his shoulders. He spied a small branch that had at one time been the top of a tree. Desperately, he grabbed for it and hung on with both hands. It provided him a temporary reprieve from the raging water.

Rusty was desperate. He had almost drowned. He was hanging onto the top limb of a cedar tree. The current was too strong for him to get across the river. He wasn't sure he could get back to land. He was going to have to do something, fast. The water raged around him, and it was increasingly more difficult to hold on to the tree. At least no one would look in the water for him, but the water was rising, and soon it would be over the tree limb. His only chance was to try to get back to land.

He let go of the tree and began to swim. The duffel bag made swimming difficult. He felt himself being pulled into the current and began to struggle in the swirling waters, which carried him wildly downstream. He crashed into the tops of trees as he tumbled along. He kept going under, swallowing water, and coming to the surface gasping for air.

He tried to make his way to shore. He had to get rid of the duffel bag, but it contained everything they had stolen. No, he needed it. He wouldn't give it up, no matter what.

Without warning, the current yanked him beneath the surface of the water. Deeper and deeper he sank. The weight on his shoulders was dragging him to a final baptism. He jerked to get the load off his back, swallowing water with each try. Finally, with a last pull, he wrenched himself free. He rushed to the surface and thrust himself into the air. His lungs filled with oxygen. As suddenly as he had propelled to the surface, he was pushed back under. Again, he had to fight his way to the top; all the while, he was hurled downstream like a piece of paper tossed into a whirlpool. Give up! That would be the easy thing to do. *No!* He kept fighting. He could make it.

He struggled to find something to hold onto, something lasting and strong. Blindly, his hand struck an object in the water. Maybe it was another log. He clung tightly to the limb. Abruptly, the log rolled over in the water. Lightning flashed, and his eyes caught sight of the object in the water. Vomit rose in his throat. He let go and was immediately swept away by the rushing current. His mind could not comprehend what his eyes had just seen. It was Dennis, he was sure of that. But half of his face was missing, and there was only an empty space where his right eye should have been. Panic gripped him. He struggled to stay afloat in the swirling water. The rain continued to pour down and lightning crashed closer than before.

Out of the Darkness

Thrashing about wildly in the swirling water, his foot finally touched bottom. Madly, he scrambled toward dry land. Freeing himself from the torrent of the stream, he collapsed, waterlogged, on the soggy ground. He lay heaving on the ground, the water lapping at his feet, and the rain beating down on his back.

He wasn't sure how long he had been there. *Had he fallen asleep?* He wasn't sure. His face and hair were caked with mud, and he was shivering from the cold rain that crashed down unrelentingly. He tried to rise, but couldn't find the strength. Clawing the ground with his hands, he slowly rose to his knees. The ooze stuck to his face and hands like flypaper. He stumbled to his feet and staggered a few steps. His legs felt like great weights. The red clay gripped his feet tightly, and he struggled to keep his balance. He tried to walk, but his feet sank in the plowed ground until it was over the top of his boots. It was no use; he couldn't escape through the field. Dejected, he sank back down, surrendering to the rain and mud.

Lightning again streaked and exploded in a dance across the sky. The thunder rumbled like a great earthquake and shook the earth. Startled by the fiery display, the exhausted man raised his head and scanned the sky. The rain still came down hard, but the lightning illuminated his surroundings for miles around. A burst struck nearby, followed by a series of flashes across the sky.

On a hill less than a hundred yards away, he could clearly make out the figure of a man. Panic overwhelmed him. In his struggle to escape the rushing water, he had almost forgotten that someone was after him. His heart pumped violently in his chest, as if trying to escape his body. His eyes darted about, searching for a means of escape.

He began to look for his weapon. *Had he lost it in the river? No, he remembered having it after he crawled to the bank.* Crawling on his hands and knees, he searched the mire until his hand hit something solid. Having the gun in his hand brought a sense of relief. He slid down to the water's edge and began to wash the mud off the barrel.

Even with the gun, there was little chance to escape. What had happened to Dennis wasn't going to happen to him. His only hope was the river. He couldn't get away through that mud, but he might be able to swim the river if he weren't so weighted down. He'd slip back in the water and let the current carry him downstream. When he found a decent place, he would swim across. He was sure he could make it. He pulled off his coat and shoes. The wind was freezing. He shivered. He tucked the gun in his belt, fastened it snugly against his stomach, and disappeared into the black, murky water.

Rusty struggled in the water. He'd always thought he was a pretty good swimmer. He remembered one spring at Lake Eerie, where the undertow had been so powerful that even the lifeguards had trouble swimming back to shore against it, but this was different. The current was coming from different directions, like a vortex dragging him down.

He tried to rest by swimming on his back, but the current slammed him about violently. The water pushed him downstream rapidly, keeping his head under water. He struggled to the surface and gasped a breath of air. He saw the bank on the far side of the river, but had no strength left to swim toward it. Slowly, he began to sink. Water filled his nostrils. He thought about quitting; quitting would be easier. Once again, he fought his way to the surface, his arms flailing wildly. He began to sink again; he thrashed about, but it was useless. Water filled his mouth and lungs. He tried to scream.

Chapter 28

On the knoll, Jake saw his prey disappearing into the swirling water. Quickly, he raised his rifle, waiting for the next flash of lightning to expose his target. It never came. The rain beat down relentlessly, making it impossible to see more than a few feet away. It seemed as if the heavens had opened up to saturate the earth and save the condemned man.

There was still one left that he could get. Rusty may have gotten away for now, but the cops would catch him if he did manage to get across the river. All this was Preacher's idea; he was the one that would have to pay. He would deal with Rusty later. Jake was close enough to walk to Preacher's house. It would be faster than going back and getting his truck. Besides, there were going to be all kinds of questions to answer.

It was only then that he began to think about what he had done. He had been so consumed with rage that his only thoughts had been revenge. *Had he done anything wrong? No! He was only catching the people that had killed his parents, his blood. They deserved to die, didn't they? No one could blame him for what he had done.*

He had to walk through the plowed field to reach the cove road. As he walked, his mind battled his conscience. *Why not— the Bible says an "eye for an eye," but "Vengeance is mine, sayth the Lord."*

More and more, his mind raced to his parents. *Why did they have to kill them? Robbing them would have been bad enough.*

They hadn't deserved to die. They never hurt anyone. Why, Lord, did you let this happen? They were fine people; there never was a better Christian than Mama. Why did God let something like this happen?

He felt so sorry for his parents. They had always worked hard, and now, when they were able to quit work and enjoy life, life had been taken away from them.

Most of all, he was sorry for himself. He remembered all the times they had been there when he needed them. He thought back to when he had been sick and throwing up. His mama would hold his head while he heaved, and afterwards wiped his face with a cold rag. There was a great deal of security there. He would never be able to ask them a question again, never seek their counsel, or have their advice to heed. It was a lonely feeling. Though he had other family, he felt orphaned. *Why hadn't he told them more often that he loved them?* Sure, they knew it, but he should have told them more. If only he had the chance again.

Jake trudged out of the plowed field, crossed a fence with two strands of barbed wire at the top, and made his way to the road. The bridge loomed ahead, dark, silent, and foreboding, a silhouette, eerily appearing and then disappearing with each flash of lightning. About forty yards west of the bridge, blue lights flashed, and a siren sounded. It was only a short distance away. At the other end of the bridge sat a patrol car. The rain had prevented him from seeing it until now. He thought about running, but the patrol car remained stationary. Through the pouring rain, he could make out the headlights of a vehicle approaching from the opposite direction. Fate was on his side, after all. The cop flashed his lights to stop the other car.

Jake eased back down the bank, out of sight. He had to get across that bridge, and he didn't have time to answer questions. He had to get to Preacher's.

Small streams ran into the river near the bridge, and during the spring rains, they overflowed the entire area. The way the water swirled under the bridge made it foolish to try to swim across here.

Out of the Darkness

He had to get to the other side. He made his way closer to the bridge abutment. Maybe he could walk across it on the outside. It was an old, two-beam bridge with steel and concrete sides. The bridge normally stood some twenty feet above the water, but because of the rain, the water was only a foot below the deck of the bridge.

He could ease into the water, grab hold of the bridge, and pull himself up on the foothold. He had fished off the old bridge many times with his father, and he knew the ledge was at least wide enough for him to walk.

He swung his rifle across his shoulder and quietly edged down the bank and into the water. The water was cold, but it was only a foot or two deep. Two more steps, and the water was above his waist. The river was plunging rapidly beneath the bridge, and he realized he would only have one chance to grab hold of the trestle. If he missed, he would be swept under the bridge and into the current. At the mercy of the river, he might be dashed into the columns of the bridge or become entangled in the trees littering the banks downstream from the bridge. Either way, the prospects weren't too promising. He had to catch hold of the bridge. The water was up to his shoulders, but his feet were still touching the ground. Just a few more feet, and he could grab the railing of the bridge. Only a few more feet—

Without warning, the rushing water jerked him toward the bridge. He had made a mistake. The whirlpool created by the water being forced to travel through a smaller opening was sucking him downward. He struggled to reach the surface.

Water filled his mouth and nose. Blindly he stabbed at the darkness in search of the bridge. His left hand poked desperately into the narrow space between the concrete that allowed water to drain from the bridge. The rough concrete tore the flesh of his hand, and the water pulled the rest of his body under the bridge. Furiously, his right hand searched for another crevice. All he could find was the solid, wet, slick surface of the bridge. He couldn't hold on with one hand any longer. With a last effort, he thrust his right hand into another space in the bridge. He clawed at the hold to secure himself to the bridge.

After what seemed like minutes, he was able to pull himself up enough that he could hold onto the bridge and rest. His arms ached, and both of his hands were bleeding from the scrapes and cuts caused by the concrete. He was lucky to be alive. If he had missed the bridge, he would have been tossed about like a squirrel in the jaws of a dog. He wasn't safe yet. He had to struggle to get his foot on the narrow ledge. After several unsuccessful efforts, he was able to get both feet on the ledge.

He was in an uncomfortable position. If he pulled himself up to hold onto the rail, someone might see him. If he stayed below the rail, he would have to inch along a little bit at a time and stick his hands between the sandpaper concrete walls. It was painfully slow. He had to be careful. The police car was only a few feet away, and he didn't want to battle the raging river again.

After only a few yards, his knees ached terribly. He should have never played football. Not only his knees, but also his hand and fingers cramped, as well. His fingertips and the back of his hands felt like raw meat.

Halfway across the bridge was a small tower. He never knew what it was for, but he knew he would have a chance to rest if he got there. He neared the tower, lightning flashed, and he saw a cop walking across the bridge from the opposite end, looking into the water, as if he expected something to be there. The only chance he had was to get to the tower before the cop spotted him. He tried to move faster, but it was a struggle to keep his balance. *What would he say if he were caught?* He looked up to see how much time he had, his foot slipped from the foothold, and he began to lose his balance. In desperation, he lunged toward the metal support that connected the tower to the bridge. He was too close to the tower and came crashing down on it with his chest. He felt a stabbing pain and knew he had broken ribs. Still, he held firmly to the bar and allowed his body to sink into the dark water and drift under the bridge. He walked his hands as far down the support as he could and hoped he wouldn't be noticed. The cop turned and walked back to the car. The heavens opened up once again, and an onslaught of rain washed everything from sight.

Unable to get a deep breath, he managed to pull himself back onto the ledge. After several minutes, he was able to cross the bridge.

When he reached the other side, he was confronted with another problem. He had to jump into the ditch and try to swim against the current or crawl along the bank in full view of the other patrol car. He had already contended with the water once and didn't care to try it again. He would have to crawl along the bank and hope that the rain prevented anyone from spotting him.

He began to crawl. His lungs felt like they would burst. Raising his hands above his head was excruciatingly painful. When he tried to use his arms to help him along, he almost screamed. He saw the front bumper of the cruiser standing above him like a sentry. He was in full view of anyone in the car that might look his direction. "No lightning now," he pleaded silently. Suddenly, the door of the patrol car swung open. His heart raced. Had he been caught? He lay quietly, trying to melt into the scenery, hoping he wouldn't be seen. The trooper got out and walked to the front of the car. He looked bored. After stretching a couple of times, he got back in the car.

He edged down the bank far enough to be out of sight, yet where he could still hold on to the grass and weeds. At last, he reached a place where the water was shallow enough that he could cross the ditch and walk in the field.

The soil wasn't plowed, so the walking was much easier. Mr. Jacobs owned this field, and he never plowed it because the soil was so wet, poor, and inhospitable to life. The soil in Booneville was rich, red clay, but this was a grayish-brown color. There were rocks just a few inches under the ground, and plants couldn't grow their roots deep.

His father had always told him you "had to have good roots to survive when the weather got rough and times got bad."

Michael Clinton Oliver

Maybe that's why nothing good would grow here in the cove. About all this land would grow was scrub cedar trees and sage grass.

He was almost there. He walked by the bend in the river, toward the spring. He needed a drink of water. Big Spring had always been one of his favorite spots. The spring emptied from the mountain near the mouth of Saltpeter Cave. Large oak trees surrounded the spring on three sides. The ridge above the spring was populated with scraggly cedars. Near the mouth, a large weeping willow commanded the area, its limbs skirting the ground, flowing like a wedding dress. Large boulders lay like giant ants, protecting their abode.

The spring water was refreshing. Strange, even with all the rain, he still felt so dry. Lying back on a rock, he surveyed his numerous injuries. The worst was his ribs. They hurt with every breath he took. He had banged his leg pretty badly on the bridge, and his hands were both sore. Still, it wasn't anything that wouldn't heal. He wondered what time it was. It was so hard to tell on such a dark night. It was probably getting close to daylight. He had to get to Preacher's before it got light. It seemed darker than before. Earlier, there had been enough lightning to see where he was walking; now the blackness made it impossible to see his path.

Chapter 29

Jake left the spring and hiked down the road. A few minutes later, Rusty emerged from the river and collapsed, exhausted, on the ground. He couldn't believe he had escaped the swift flowing stream. It was almost as if the river had toyed with him, and then, when it tired of play, had flung him on dry land. He lay there for several minutes, inhaling deeply. He was exhausted, but more determined than ever to survive. He had lost what they had stolen, but he was alive.

Finally, he picked up his gun and staggered to the road. He, too, stopped at the spring for a quick drink and trudged down the road. Lightning once again lit up the sky, and he saw someone walking up the road only a couple hundred yards away. *Now*, Rusty thought, *it's my time to do the hunting.*

Ahead in the road, Jake's side ached with pain. His ribs were broken. He remembered when he had cracked his ribs in football his senior year in high school; the pain was much the same, only worse. He continued with no thought of stopping. He was almost there, and nothing was going to stop him.

He crossed Dry Creek Bridge and left the main road, taking a shortcut across a field. The rain continued to fall, but he seemed not to notice.

He stopped to rest for a moment at the entrance to Clark Grove Cemetery. He thought about walking around the graves, but he was hurting, and the shortest distance to Preacher's house was straight through.

The ground took on an unearthly feeling. The soil in the graveyard felt spongy, like he was walking on a mattress. He always hated the way it felt, as if you were going to fall into a grave yourself. The ground was so porous that with every step he expected to sink farther into the earth.

Silent granite soldiers guarded the dead. Silhouetted by occasional flashes of lightning, they served as sentinels over the graveyard. Lined in rows, they related tales of remarkable deeds, undying love, and prayers that served as sonnets to the long forgotten dead.

Jake leaned against a tall monument to rest. Breathing was difficult. Every step he took caused agonizing pain in his side. He dreaded each breath, fearing the stabbing pain that would accompany it.

After escaping the mushy graveyard, he returned to the road. The footing was better, and his steps became quicker. He rounded the curve and saw a light on in Preacher's house. He made his way for the front door.

Chapter 30

Preacher had been waiting to hear from the boys. It was late. He was sure something had gone wrong, bad wrong. He paced back and forth, rubbing his hands together to try to get warm. He felt like a stranger in his own home, a visitor, ill at ease and out of place among familiar surroundings.

"Damn," he said aloud. He didn't need any more trouble, that was certain. *What could have happened? He should have gone with them.* "Damn. Damn. Damn."

If they were caught, maybe they wouldn't squeal on him. No, some of them would turn state's evidence. He'd kill himself before he went to prison. Damn that Ben Patton. Maybe get a rope and hang himself in the barn. They said Billy Forte's eyes had popped clean out of his head when he had hanged himself from that big oak tree down by the Blue Hole. No, he didn't have the guts to do that.

Preacher was startled by the sound of someone stepping on the porch.

"That you, boys?" he asked. He waited, but there was no answer.

"Rusty, is that you?" he hollered, getting more anxious.

The door crashed open, splintering into parts. Preacher reached for his shotgun. He grabbed the stock of the gun, but was wrestled to the ground before he could aim and fire. He fought to gain control, but was thrown across the room and onto the bed.

He struggled to get up. He felt as if he were caught in a vice. A punch caught him flush in the nose. He heard it break. Thick, sticky blood poured from his nose and ran into his mouth. He spat to try to clear his throat. Once again, he was grabbed and thrown across the room. He crashed into the table, breaking the coffee cups atop it. As he tried to regain his balance, he fell into the kerosene heater.

The heater tipped over and exploded in a ball of fire. Flames erupted all around him. His shirt was on fire. The heat seared his face. He tried to run, but was tackled from behind. The fire raced up the dried wallpaper, engulfed the walls, and soon spread to the whole house. The smoke was thick. He coughed. Unable to see, he beat at the flames with his hands. He thrashed about, fiercely trying to free himself—kicking and hitting at the person who had him pinned to the floor. He was suffocating. He couldn't last much longer.

He didn't know if there was a way to get out of the inferno, even if he could get loose. The man kept hitting him. He tried to run. The man caught him and pulled him back to the back of the house. He was losing consciousness. His hand searched for something to hold. He was hurled back across a table into the wall. He tried to pick himself off the floor, but his leg gave way.

"Broke," he said aloud. He slumped to the floor. His hand felt something, an iron poker. He grabbed it with both hands and swung blindly. He was surprised that halfway through his swing, he landed solidly. He squinted to try to see what he'd hit. The smoke was so thick he couldn't tell. He might have a chance to get out of this blazing hell. He stumbled forward, but the smoke was too thick. He collapsed to his knees after a few feet. The smoke was unbearable, choking the life out of his body.

He rolled over on his back. Someone was above him. He swung the poker and again felt the jar as it struck the man's leg. He swung again and connected in the mid-section, the man doubled over. One final blow across the head would do it, he thought. He raised the poker with both hands.

Outside, Rusty arrived at the burning house. He tried to get in, but the flames drove him back. He saw the men struggling in the smoke and aimed his gun. Before he had a chance to pull the trigger, Shelby emerged from the shadows and fired into his face. The blast from the .357 propelled Rusty across the porch. A flash of light in the dark, explosions went off in his head, but there was no sound, only the flames. Red, everything was red, and he fell. His body twisted around in the dance of death, his arms and legs flailed about before he fell off the porch, face first onto the muddy ground.

Shelby stared at his body before she moved toward the house. Carrie had called, saying someone had murdered Ben Patton and his wife. She knew Rusty was involved. She also knew he would be at Preacher's. She got her gun and went straight to Preacher's house. She parked down the road and waited outside in the rain, protected by the dark. She was surprised when she saw Jake Patton stumble up the road, but she remained in the shadows, unsure what to do. Her uncertainty vanished as she saw Rusty approach, gun in hand, and take aim at Jake in the flaming building.

He hadn't even seen her. She wished he had known who shot him. She wanted him to know. She hoped he felt her pain. She didn't have time to do anything but step out of the shadows and fire. She was afraid she might miss, but her aim was true. She held the gun just like Rusty taught her. Bam! It was so loud. Her ears were still ringing.

Preacher hesitated when he heard gunfire. The hesitation cost him his life. Jake grabbed Preacher's leg and jerked with all the strength he had left in his body.

Preacher's head crashed to the floor. He grabbed the poker, but before he could swing, he was battered by a fury of punches. Jake took the poker and shoved it against Preacher's neck, choking him with his own poker. All around him was black. Smoke billowed through the room. Preacher tried to cough, but air wouldn't fill his lungs. He pushed with all his power, but the poker never moved. Steadily, it began to twist until the point was just above Preacher's belt buckle. Panic flooded his mind. His eyes bulged; the veins in his neck stood taut. With a final thrust, the poker ripped Preacher's flesh and buried itself deep in his abdomen. Blood gushed from the wound. His arms lost control. He wanted to speak, but there was only darkness.

Chapter 31

The house was totally engulfed in flames as Shelby rushed into the furnace. It was hard to make out anything in the dense smoke. She crawled along the floor. Jake was probably already dead. *Why hadn't she acted sooner?* Pieces of burning roof fell in around her. Toward the back of the room, she saw Jake lying on the floor, trying to crawl out of the flames.

She rushed through the flames and grabbed him. Tears ran down her cheeks. *Why hadn't she acted sooner?* She tried to help him stand, but he was weak and battered. He slumped on hands and knees, unable to stand.

She grabbed him around the waist and tried to pick him up. He was dead weight. She strained with all her might, but could not get him to his feet. She couldn't breath. The heat was intense, searing her face and hands. Smoke filled her lungs and stung her eyes. More of the roof caved in. In seconds, the entire structure would collapse.

Jake tried to crawl, but toppled face-first on the floor. He was unconscious, maybe dead. The heat was too intense. She had to escape. She rolled Jake over, got both hands underneath his arms, and tried to drag him. He was too heavy. She was barely able to budge him.

She pulled so hard that she fell backwards. His body moved a few inches. She got up and pulled, once again crashing to the floor. She kept repeating the process, inching closer to the door. The flames grew hotter. A large portion of the ceiling collapsed, sending sparks and flames across the room. Flames erupted on her face. Her hair was on fire. She beat at the flames with her bare hands, finally extinguishing the blaze.

She tried to pick Jake up again. The pain from her burnt hands was too much to bear. She got underneath his arms with the crook of her elbows and fell backwards. She felt the fresh air just outside the door. She tried to get a breath. Her chest heaved. "Please, help me, dear God," she pleaded.

A beam from the ceiling came crashing down, landing on Jake's right leg. She kicked at the burning timber until she got it off his body. Once more, she hooked Jake's arms with her elbows and fell backwards. When she landed, she found herself outside, on the porch. The rotting wood porch sloped downward, which made it easier for her to drag his body away from the fire.

Once outside, Jake began to cough and moan. Finally, he opened his eyes and looked at Shelby. He wanted to ask her why? How? A slight smile crossed his lips, and his eyes closed again. The house was totally consumed by the flames. The rain had finally stopped. The sun was coming up, and the long night was over.

Michael - Melody - Judd

MOliverBooks.Com

Melody03@hotmail.Com